Sensuous Burgundy

Barbara Delinsky

SENSUOUS BURGUNDY

WHEELER
PUBLISHING, INC.
ROCKLAND, MA

★ AN AMERICAN COMPANY ★

14893257

Copyright © 1981 by Barbara Delinsky

Published in Large Print by arrangement with HarperPaperbacks, a division of HarperCollins Publishers, Inc. in the United States and Canada.

Wheeler Large Print Book Series.

Set in 16 pt. Plantin.

Library of Congress Cataloging-in-Publication Data

Delinsky, Barbara.
   Sensuous burgundy / Barbara Delinsky.
      p.   cm.—(Wheeler large print book series)
    ISBN 1-56895-393-3
    1. Large type books. I. Title. II. Series.
  [PS3554.E4427S43 1996]
  813'.54—dc21   96-45009
                                               CIP

To my husband, Stephen

One

She was the image of composure as she entered the crowded courtroom and started toward the prosecutor's table. Her gray suit, straight-skirted and seasonally chic for January in New England, made its intended understatement. Her sleek black hair was drawn into a sedate coil at the nape of the neck. She wore a minimum of makeup, highlighted by the deep burgundy tone on her lips, which matched that on the tips of her tapered fingers. The briefcase which swung by her side as her slim legs carried her forward, past row after row of hardwood benches, spoke of the efficiency for which she had become known. Yet the slight hush which Laura Grandine's appearance caused reminded her that as a woman, no less a lawyer, she was as much on trial as the accused.

"Some crowd for a simple arraignment," she observed under her breath to Sandy Chatfield, as she slid into a chair beside him. Darkly blond as his name suggested, the good-looking state trooper, assigned to the case from the start, was an invaluable assistant as well as a friend. Now Laura cast him a questioning glance, her blue eyes reflecting surprise at the turnout of students, family, press, and others to witness the brief proceeding.

Sandy looked at Laura with unabashed admiration. "They've braved the ice and wind just to see you in action, Laura." He grinned, winking in his boyish way, then growing more serious as

1

he leaned closer. "Actually, there is word going around that the boy has retained a new lawyer."

Immediately, Laura gave him her full attention, ignoring the notes which she had begun to remove from her briefcase. "Are you serious? You mean, Fritz MacKenzie won't be representing him?"

"Looks that way."

In a spontaneous gesture she put a hand on her friend's sleeve. "But why? MacKenzie is one of the more capable lawyers in western Massachusetts. What happened?" Amazed as she was by the turn of events, Laura's face remained calm.

The trooper arched an eyebrow in echo of his shrug, his voice hardening. "Who knows! Rumor has it that the family has turned to some high-powered guy from Boston—"

"Excuse me." A deep voice interrupted the interchange. "Assistant District Attorney Grandine?" The velvet-smooth sound brought Laura's head up with a start, her eyes riveted to the chocolate-brown orbs which were studying her.

Sheer force of habit drew her out of her chair, impelling her to offer her right hand to the stranger. Instinctively, she knew that the figure before her, towering over her in spite of her three-inch heels, was something other than the traditional court officer, visiting observer, or press representative. The attitude of self-command, conveyed by the firm set of his square jaw and the studied relaxation of his features, held a special significance, as did the vague familiarity of the ruggedly handsome face itself. As Laura struggled to make the identification, she was unaware that her brow had furrowed lightly. In response, the

2

man before her broke into an open smile, his hand retaining its warm grip long after the handshake had stilled.

"I'm Maxwell Kraig. I'll be representing Jonathan Stallway." Dazzled by the even whiteness of his powerful smile, Laura steadied herself to cope with this revelation of his identity.

Denying the pulsing knot that had suddenly formed in her stomach, she returned his smile with her own, equally as open and conveying a self-confidence she was far from feeling. "This *is* an honor, Mr. Kraig," she said softly and evenly, as she had willed. "Your reputation precedes you. I look forward to working with you." Then, abruptly remembering that they were not alone, and momentarily disturbed to have forgotten it in the first place, she disengaged her hand from his and gestured to her left. "I'd like you to meet Sandy Chatfield. He is my state trooper assigned to this case." Her use of the possessive had been subconscious, though she was to later regard Sandy as a bodyguard of sorts. Now, however, it was peripheral vision that told her that Sandy had risen, her eyes held entranced by those before her as she made the introduction. "Sandy . . . Maxwell Kraig."

Only then did the attorney's gaze flicker, his scrutiny more shrewd as he extended his hand. "Trooper Chatfield, it's my pleasure," he acknowledged politely, his eyes sharp and assessing. Laura had always thought of Sandy as a tall man, yet, standing opposite Maxwell Kraig, he seemed suddenly smaller.

"How do you do, Mr. Kraig," Sandy responded tautly. "Welcome to Northampton. You must have just arrived." He spoke quickly,

3

his distrust of the suave lawyer's lawyer not hidden by the thickness of his New England twang.

This time there was a suspicious slash to the corners of his well-formed mouth when Maxwell Kraig grinned. "I didn't think you fellows *would* miss much," he granted. "I drove out from Boston this morning. It's made for an early day, but I was able to use the travel time to plot my defense. I understand—" he switched his view, with instant effect, to Laura's deceptively composed features—"that Miss Grandine is a formidable adversary. It's not every day that I have the opportunity to try a case opposite a woman, let alone such a distractingly beautiful one."

Impaled once more by his gaze, Laura felt herself stripped of all defense, sensing immediately the strength of his physical mien on his victims—witness and juror alike. Yet, something in his words, a subtle challenge just short of patronization, spurred her on.

"Flattery will get you nowhere with this particular woman, Mr. Kraig, though a few more smiles like that will tip me off as to your charm before the jury. You wouldn't want to reveal all your secrets, now," she chided softly, any anger at his reference to her sex having melted beneath the glow of his warm brown eyes.

A darker eyebrow arched mischievously. "I doubt there's much chance of that, though I will take your warning to heart," he jibed, a vaguely sensuous light passing from his eyes to hers, turning to faint amusement as Laura unsuccessfully sought a response. It was a mixed blessing when Sandy touched her elbow. For just as she was saved from having to provide a witty rejoinder, she had been so totally entranced by his compelling personage that she jumped in surprise at the sudden reminder of the other man, whom she had momentarily forgotten. Blushing, she turned to follow her friend's gaze to the doorway in which the defendant now stood.

"If you'll excuse me, Miss Grandine, Trooper Chatfield . . ." The dark head nodded to each in turn before the tall figure turned and headed toward his client. Laura watched him go, released now from his eye hold long enough to examine the rest of him. What she saw was as compelling as those eyes had been magnetic.

Dressed in an immaculately tailored navy three-piece suit, the man was as lean as he was tall, broad shoulders belying a slimness of waist and hips which showed itself in the litheness of his gait as he crossed the room. A crisp white shirt edged beyond the cuffs of his jacket and again above its collar, there shadowed by the thick brown hair which tapered neatly to that length. Laura had to admit that Maxwell Kraig was, beyond a doubt one of the most handsome men she had ever seen, let alone opposed.

"Laura . . . hey, Laura . . ." The whispered nudge from the vicinity of her elbow brought her abruptly back from her daydreams. With an almost imperceptible shake of the head, Laura looked toward Sandy, whose annoyance was obvious. Hurriedly, she resumed her seat, unaware at what point Sandy had done so.

There was open reproachment in the words he whispered. "Ms. Prosecutor, what was *that* all about?"

Slowly, her heightened color eased as she

5

regained her composure, defensively turning to the papers before her. "What was *what* all about?" she countered with deftly manufactured nonchalance.

Sandy's voice was an impatient whisper. "Come on, Laura. This is old Sandy you're dealing with. Old hawk-eye trooper Sandy," he chided. "Those looks passing between the two of you . . . do you two have something going?"

"You've got to be kidding," she retorted playfully, sensing that the only chance she had of denying his observation was through sheer wit. "No way. I've never met the man before. But I knew he looked familiar. That face on the front page of a newspaper would *have* to make an impression. And he obviously expected a reaction. I thought I put on a good show. After all, it does no good to antagonize the defense," she added with a deliberate chuckle, putting an end to the discussion as she feigned concentration on her papers.

Although Sandy knew her well enough to take the hint, his words echoed in her mind. What *had* that been about, she wondered, her eyes sightlessly skimming the typewritten notes at her fingertips. Readily she admitted her surprise and excitement at working opposite such a renowned trial attorney. Maxwell Kraig had not only tried some of the most challenging and controversial cases in recent years, but he had become a best-selling author with his dramatic analyses of his more spectacular cases. Yes, Laura was the first to confess pleasure at this opportunity to observe him in the courtroom. Yet had there been a deeper significance to the visual charge that had passed between them?

With a flicker of her long, dark eyelashes, Laura dismissed the possibility. She was a professional. In her capacity as a lawyer she had never allowed sexual enticements to sidetrack her. As a female she had had to work too hard in this predominantly male group to allow for any nonprofessional behavior. Sandy's suggestion was absurd, she assured herself, yet she couldn't keep her eyes from wandering toward the defense table, where the attorney and his client had already seated themselves.

In profile, as she now saw him, the man was as strong-featured as he had been head-on, his forehead sturdy beneath the swath of wavy hair which fell casually upon it, his nose straight and aristocratic, his lips firm yet sensual, his chin set and suggestive of a stubbornness which Laura could only imagine.

As though her gaze had tapped him on the shoulder, his head swiveled slowly toward her, his lips twitching up into the semblance of a smirk, a maddening hint of arrogance in his deep brown gaze. Ironically, his expression was just enough to raise her hackles as a woman—and remind her that her womanhood had no role in this courtroom. In a deliberately casual movement, she forced herself to face forward, just as the court officer intoned his solemn call.

"Hear ye, hear ye . . . " So it began—the arraignment at which Jonathan Stallway answered to the charge of the first-degree murder of Susan Oliverri. A mere ten minutes later the proceeding ended, the defendant pleading not guilty to the charge as read, and the prosecution successfully arguing against bail.

"Nice going, Laura." The friendly voice was

at her ear the instant the judge returned to his chambers and court was recessed. Ever her champion, Sandy was usually all the encouragement she needed. This time, however, she wondered if it would be enough, as she gathered her papers together and returned them to her briefcase. The past three years in the district attorney's office had prepared her well for the arraignment procedure; the actual trial was another matter. And, in this particular case, with this particular charge, this particular defendant, and now, this particular defense attorney, Laura knew herself to be in a completely different league. Hiding the flicker of apprehension that momentarily clouded her gaze, she stood and straightened her shoulders.

"Laura." A hand at her right elbow drew her attention. "Good work! I had every confidence you could pull it off."

The suspicious glimmer in the D.A.'s eye as he regarded her tipped Laura to his deeper meaning. "Frank," she accused in a soft, sing-song tone, her blue eyes flashing a gentle warning of their own, "you knew, didn't you, you devil!" Franklin Potter shot her a guilty grin, his ruddy complexion growing even more so by the minute. "Why didn't you warn me?" she hissed in an urgent whisper. Only with this man, whom she had known for so many years, could she confess to any breach in her self-confidence. Frank understood her well.

"Would it have helped?" His voice was low toned and infinitely compassionate. Appreciative of his candor, a spontaneous smile overspread Laura's features.

"No." She laughed softly, at herself as much

as at him. "I suppose not. But you could have prepared me—"

"I'd like to do that now, Laura, but I'm on my way to that convention in Florida," he interrupted apologetically. "I'll see you tomorrow night, though, won't I?"

"But Frank—" the slender woman protested, only to be silenced once more.

"Later, Laura. I'll tell you anything you need to know. Now, I believe you have a deskful of cases to attend to?" he reminded her firmly, once again the man in command.

Standing as they were at the front of the very slowly emptying courtroom, Laura had no choice but to accept his dismissal. "Yes, sir," she murmured smartly, then raised her voice a bit. "Have a good trip, Mr. District Attorney." Franklin Potter parried her go-jump-in-the-lake look with an indulgent grin, then turned and made his way out of the courtroom. In an instant Sandy Chatfield's hand was at Laura's elbow to escort her likewise. With a small group milling about the defense table, she had no further look at her adversary before she dutifully gripped her briefcase and acceded to the trooper's suggestion.

Laura carried herself confidently, aware of the glances cast her way by the curious as she retraced her earlier route, unwinding only after she had reached the privacy of her own office, which was tucked compactly among the others in the basement of the courthouse building. Sinking into the comfortable leather desk chair she'd wheedled out of the building department, she was grateful that her trooper-in-attendance had had other matters to attend to, leaving her alone to digest the morning's events.

9

Maxwell Kraig—what was it, she wondered idly, about his name that raised the status of the case a peg or two? Then immediately she chided herself. This was a homicide, regardless of the lawyers involved, and as such was a heinous crime to prosecute. A young girl was dead, allegedly slain by her jealous boyfriend, and the presence of Maxwell Kraig should have no effect whatsoever on the gravity of the case.

But it did. Laura was not that naive as to believe otherwise. It would mean, for starters, more television and press coverage. It would mean greater crowds in attendance during each step of the proceedings. It would mean the ultimate challenge for Laura to keep one step ahead of the reputedly keen and acutely insightful and calculating legal mind of this defense attorney. And, if this day was any precursor of those to come, it would mean the greatest for Laura to maintain her wits before this devastatingly commanding figure of a man.

In hindsight she recalled the touch of his gaze, momentarily enjoying its hold before angrily shaking herself free of its memory. Annoyed with the train of her thought, a glance around her office brought back reality. It was all here, plain and unembellished—the desk at which she'd sat for long hours preparing cases, the file cabinets holding folder upon folder of miscellaneous data, the bookshelf containing her own legal volumes plus those she regularly borrowed from the library, the walls bearing the Daumier reproductions she had picked up in Paris. This was her life, this office, this job. As a lawyer, she had begun to establish herself.

A soft smile played on her lips as she recalled

her pride when she'd phoned her father to tell him of this, her first murder case. He had shared that pride, thereby magnifying it. At that moment Laura knew that all the razzing she'd taken from her family and friends, all the teasing and criticism she'd weathered through law school, all the skepticism she'd had to face when she had first arrived in Northampton—it all had been nothing compared to the feeling of satisfaction she now savored. She wondered what her dad would say when he learned who the defense attorney was!

But enough! With a determined straightening of her back, she willed the darkly entrancing face of Maxwell Kraig out of her mind. Franklin Potter had been correct—there had been too much work put aside during the preparation for the grand jury two days ago, then the arraignment this morning, to be wasting time on irrelevant musings.

She draped her jacket over the back of her chair in the slightly overheated office and withdrew the folder labelled Commonwealth v. Stallway from her briefcase, replaced it in the file cabinet and withdrew those others that demanded her immediate attention.

Fuelled by the exhilaration of the morning's proceeding, she stopped only briefly for a late lunch. Past experience told her that given the overlong hours she'd put in during the last week, she would collapse of exhaustion before the day was out. But for now the adrenaline was running fast and free, and she knew enough to take advantage of it before the fall.

It was late afternoon when she raised her eyes from the transcript she'd been studying. She always worked with her door open, reluctant to isolate herself from the rest of humanity more than the intense concentration on her work necessitated. Now something intangible distracted her. In a gesture of the fatigue which had just begun to be felt, she raised a forefinger to her forehead as she looked toward the door. There, lounging casually, his lengthy form dominating the frame, was Maxwell Kraig. Surprised that he was still in town, the arraignment having been completed hours ago, and thoroughly unprepared for his appearance at her own office, Laura was momentarily tongue-tied, recapturing her composure only as the man uncoiled his length from the door jamb and entered the office.

"I'm sorry, Mr. Kraig," she offered softly, covering her puzzlement as he quietly closed the door, then leaned against it, one hand thrust deep into his pants pocket, the other propped on the doorknob. "Have you been waiting to see me?" Her voice did not betray her. She was as poised as she could ever hope to be.

He hesitated just for a moment; then his deep tone assailed her with its richness as it had done earlier in the day. "You didn't really think you'd get away from me that easily, did you, Miss Grandine?"

Refusing to be put so quickly on the defensive, she ignored his suggestive overtone. "Please do come in," she mocked gently, "and shut the door behind you, if you'd be so kind." She paused, enjoying the flicker of amusement on the face of her one-man audience, before getting to the point. "Thank you. Now, what can I do for you, counselor?" Her three years of dealing with often arrogantly chauvinistic attorneys stood her in good stead. As long as she could convince herself that Maxwell Kraig was no different from the others, she would do just fine.

To her dismay the man straightened slightly and offered mocking applause. "That was an excellent performance this morning, an even better one just now," he drawled before relaxing once more against the door. "Are you always as polished?" His warm brown eyes never left hers.

"I try," she answered evenly, an easy smile playing on her lips. "After all, it's part of my job."

"Ah-hah, and you *are* very professional, aren't you?"

Laura wondered whether he was purposely trying to bait her, and this suspicion gave her an added measure of patience. "Mr. Kraig, as one of the most prominent and able lawyers in the state, I *know* that you have already researched me. So let me ask you—do your sources report me as being very professional?" Satisfied that she had scored a point, Laura sat back, her hands draped comfortably over the arms of her chair.

His eyes narrowed as he readily answered her challenge. "Yes, I'm told that you are totally professional. But I always reserve final judgment until I've seen for myself."

Not quite prepared to follow up the last, Laura held his gaze unwaveringly. "And what else, Mr. Kraig? What other goodies did your—ah— sources dig up?"

"Let me see." He rolled his eyes skyward as he prolonged the anticipation. When he looked back down at her, there was definite amusement etched in the lines radiating from those all-enveloping eyes. "Age twenty-eight. B.A., Mount Holyoke, J.D., Cornell. Assistant District

Attorney, Hampshire County, three years. Hard worker. Tough prosecutor. Shrewd bargainer. Very straight-laced." And added gleam in his eye accompanied the lowering of his voice at the last phrase. Once more, Laura chose to ignore the bait.

"Certainly you know that this is my first homicide?" she volunteered. It occurred to her to wonder why she had wanted to add this information to the dossier. Surely she would rather have been able to tell him that she had already under her belt some of the same experience on which he had built his own career over the last twelve years. Yet she was neither a pompous nor a presumptuous person, and perhaps it was this that she had wished to convey. For an instant she feared that her forthrightness had held an implicit plea for mercy. Then as quickly as this thread entered her mind, she chased it out. She was a good lawyer, one who needed neither mercy nor compassion to win a case.

"That is correct. But then, Miss Grandine, you appear to be intimidated by neither new experiences nor new faces." The reference was obvious, though in this Laura had to congratulate herself on the deception. She did feel clearly intimidated by this man who stood so boldly before her. Yet it was an intimidation which had little to do with the law. Her thoughts had barely begun to ponder this situation when he caught her up short.

"Is Sandy Chatfield your personal protector?" For the first time Laura felt the force of his direct examination. When he wanted an answer, she realized with little amusement and definite mental note, he knew how to get it.

"Sandy is a good worker and a friend. If you're

asking whether I am involved personally with him"—her blue eyes flashed spiritedly as she returned his candor with her own—"the answer is no. I don't make a practice of mixing my professional with my personal life. But surely, Mr. Kraig, your sources told you that. Isn't that what is meant by very straight-laced?" Despite his attempts to disconcert her, Laura enjoyed the gentle sparring, gaining boldness as she went on. "Is that why you are holding that door shut? Are you worried that my trooper will barge in to defend my virtue?" A gentle giggle rippled through her lips and into the air. "Yes, I suppose good old Sandy would do just that." Then, glancing back at the more dubious look on Maxwell Kraig's face, she once again took charge. "Please, Mr. Kraig"—she motioned with her hand toward the seat on the opposite side of her desk—"have a seat. Sandy is otherwise occupied for the remainder of the day, although I can't guarantee that there will be no other interruptions." A humorous smile lingered on her lips as she tacked the last on whimsically.

Slowly and with an air of self-confidence, he stepped from the door and moved gracefully forward. "Thank you, Miss—would you mind if we dropped the formality? I really would prefer you to call me Max." He was strangely earnest in his request, as though it meant a great deal to him to be on a first-name basis with her; Laura, the last one to stand on ceremony, readily complied.

"Max? It's Laura then." She smiled warmly, unaware of the captivating picture she made when she was as suddenly relaxed as she now felt. The occasional wisp of black hair had

15

escaped from its knot as the day had progressed, and now these loose tendrils softened her face, complimenting the faint pinkness on her cheeks. Max, too, now seemed more relaxed, in a different more genuine way than the calculated calmness of earlier moments.

"You handle yourself well for a small-town girl, Laura. You must have had experience handling overbearing men from the big city." The self-deprecation did not fool her for a minute; he was enjoying himself as much as she was.

"You're right. I *have* had a lot of practice. A woman in this job has to convince people that she is a lawyer first, then a woman. It's been . . . a challenge." She smiled, recalling other words she had used to describe the situation. "Men seem to think that a woman who enters this profession is looking solely for male companionship." Now her own candor surprised her.

"What are you looking for, Laura?" he asked warmly. Once again she felt the melting effect of those brown eyes as they blanketed her.

She didn't hesitate. "I'm looking for a successful career. I want experience, not on paper, but in the courtroom. I'd like to become a good trial lawyer. At this point, that's all."

"And do you feel that the two—lawyer and woman—are incompatible?" His voice had a caressive quality, soothing in its way yet oddly disconcerting.

"Not at all," she countered quickly, lowering her eyes to trace a tapered forefinger with the thumb and fingers of the other hand. "I just don't take relationships lightly. And I realize that if I behave in this office as a female first, my chances

16

of being accepted as a lawyer will be forever put second. I don't want that."

Her thick black lashes lifted as she looked again at Max. One elbow was flexed on the arm of his chair, a hand subconsciously rubbing the roughness of his jaw, as though he too were faced with the dilemma. Laura caught herself just short of empathy. He was a man! It was he of whom *she* had to beware! The ghost of a sad smile touched her lips. There were times when she tired of playing the asexual professional; this was one of them. Impulsively, she gave rein to her very feminine curiosity.

"Tell me about yourself. You had a head start on me. *My* detectives are only getting to work now." She smirked.

"Chatfield?" The dark eyebrow arched, becoming lost behind the lock of wavy hair that had fallen progressively lower on his forehead as the day had worn on, giving him a decidedly more youthful look.

Laura nodded with a grin of concession. "Among other things, yes, Sandy does that type of research. Why don't you save him some trouble?"

A contrived sigh preceded his reply, his long legs now stretched casually before him, crossed at the ankles. Laura's eye caught on his well-polished loafers, another surprisingly independent touch for a man in the legal establishment, which notoriously saved its accolades for the crusty old gentlemen whose wardrobes bespoke of an earlier decade and who, though brilliant and outspoken in the field itself, were relatively invisible as individuals. Perhaps Max did have more going for him than a fine legal mind. Laura

17

blushed. But then she had known that since their first encounter this morning.

"Please," he chided, raising a hand in feigned protest, "no blushing *before* I begin. That sort of thing can bode ill for a fellow's ego," he quipped. Then noting the even deeper color his comment had inspired, her mercifully proceeded. Laura was surprised that he kept his gaze to the floor, an almost self-conscious gesture which was thoroughly endearing. She found herself listening intently as he rattled off his biographical data.

"Born New York City, thirty-nine years ago next month. B.A., Princeton. J.D., Harvard Law School. Two years, Legal Services, Bronx, New York. Subsequent establishment of the law offices of Maxwell Kraig and Associates." He paused, only then directing his gaze to his listener. "Trial practice consisting primarily of felony cases. Author, *Eleventh-Street Defense.*" An eye-brow lifted. "Reported to be a very eligible bachelor, thought to frequent many of the East Coast's most chi-chi night spots."

There was an abrupt silence as the listing ceased. Laura remained immobile, held by those suddenly familiar brown pools. Trained to catch the slightest innuendo as her job demanded, she heard herself question him, repeating his words. "Reported to be?"

It was a long time before Max responded, and when he did, there was a slight tensing of his features. "That seems to be all that matters . . . too often . . . " His deep voice trailed off, as he stood and walked slowly around the room, absently studying the prints on the walls. The break gave Laura a chance to recover from this injection of bitterness into a life story which should, by all reasonable measures, hold nothing but gratification.

As she watched his dark back, he dug both hands into his trouser pockets, his posture suggestive of a reluctant resignation which she could not fathom. Instinctively, and totally as a woman, she prodded him.

"I don't understand, Max." Her voice was soft; she had no idea of the sensuality of the sound which met his ears, drawing first his head, then his entire body, around until he faced her, then approached, slowly. There was an initial fierceness in his expression, which gentled rapidly as he neared.

"For a man, too, there can be a conflict between the professional and the personal. Yes, I have attained a fair level of legal success, but with it has come a distortion of any personal life I may have wished. At this point I often wonder whether there *is* a private Maxwell Kraig or whether the celebrity Maxwell Kraig—I didn't mention the television programs, panel discussions, and testimonials I am forced to endure—" he interjected with a heavy dose of sarcasm "— is the only one the world can see . . . the only one that remains after all."

Laura was astonished by the raw hurt that glittered in his eyes, the sadness that escaped from some unseen depth to tug at her. She had not known the man for more than a few hours, yet she sensed that he had opened up to her in a way in which he rarely, if ever, did. There had been an immediate rapport between the two of them. She felt oddly close to this man who had been a total stranger up until this very morning.

Sensing her thoughts, Max shook his head

19

gently. "I'm sorry. You seem to have a strange effect on me," he murmured, as he looked down at her. Now only inches from her chair, he had begun to have a strange effect on her also. For the first time, she noted the muscled span of his thigh as his pocketed hand pulled the fine fabric snugly around it. She sensed the power of his body as her eyes slowly lifted, following the tapering-out from his waist to a solid expanse of chest revealed by the thrust-back jacket. His face, strong and handsome, held a mystery that beckoned to her irresistibly.

Helpless to move, and unaware of the allure of her own slightly parted lips as her head tilted sharply up at him, she watched, mesmerized, as he bent over and rested one large hand on either arm of her chair.

For an eternity he remained with his face mere inches from hers, his breathing deep and steady, its warmth further intoxicating her reeling senses. Time was suspended. She was under his spell and at his mercy. Her gaze clung to his eyes as they traced the line of her nose, then swung over the faint hollows of her cheeks to her ears, returning along her jawline to rest on her lips, moist and sweet, waiting for his with an eagerness which would have startled her, had she been cognizant of it.

Ever so slowly he succumbed to her lure, lowering his head until his lips feather-touched hers, first with a lightness that barely tantalized, then with growing persuasion, until her own initial shyness was replaced by a response that matched his in a searching and caressing she had never before experienced. New sensitivities awakened with each shift of his lips. Swept into the vortex of his passion, she allowed, sampled, then returned the play of his tongue, until, breathing raggedly, he drew it, his lips, then his head back to look down upon her.

The end of the ecstasy brought Laura hurtling back to earth. Yet the reality to which she returned was a far cry from that she had left moments before. This master of seduction had, with his lips alone, led her on a breathtaking journey toward an irrevocably altered reality. This new reality was a burning desire for the resumption of his kiss. It was an aching need that quivered uncontrollably within her. It held an awesome awareness that frightened her as it beckoned.

Perhaps sensing this, Max straightened, then leaned back against a corner of her desk, one leg draped over the edge, the other stretched out to give him balance.

"Which will it be, Laura," he offered gently, "lawyer or woman? Or has the fine line between the two become blurred?"

It took Laura a moment to reorient herself. Then as outwardly calm as he, she smiled. "No way, counselor. The woman just dropped in for a quick visit. Had I known she were coming, I would have insisted you left that door"—she cocked her head in its direction—"open. I can assure you that she won't be by again." It was a guarantee she wanted desperately to believe. "Now," she continued for Max's benefit, "is there any other business to attend to?" Pleased with what she felt sure attested to her recovery from the throes of passion, she was taken aback by Max's follow-up.

"Have dinner with me tonight, Laura." Huskiness lingered in his tone.

There was no hesitancy in her response. "No, Max."

"Why not? Do you have other plans?" His gaze challenged her gently.

Slowly, she shook her head, her eyes leaving his for the moment. "No, I have no plans. But I won't go out with you."

"Why not?"

"Do you really think it's a wise idea?" She threw the question back at him. Where the tactic had worked earlier, now it failed.

"I'm the one who's doing the asking this time, Laura," he insisted. "Why won't you join me for a bite to eat?"

"I'm tired, for one thing." She stalled, her gaze now flickering to her desk in search of some other excuse.

"We can make it an early dinner," he persisted.

"But I still have too much to do here."

His tone lowered, taking on that caressive quality that threatened to rekindle those strange feelings within her. "You have to work late. You have to get to bed early. Which is it, Laura? Or . . . is it something else?"

Swallowing hard, Laura faced him head-on, her eyes testifying to the truth of her words. "We have a professional relationship. And, if you recall your own researcher's report, I am very straight-laced. I won't risk a personal involvement with you." She knew her argument to be aimed as much for her own ears as for his.

"A simple dinner? Is that really such a personal involvement?"

"Please," she hurried on, determined to lay

her last cards on the table, regardless of the tactical merit of the move, "I . . . lost control a minute ago. You must have sensed that. I can't afford to lose control again, not after I've worked so hard. I'm sorry, I'm not quite as sophisticated as the luxury versions you must be used to. I can't just turn it on and off. But I'm a lawyer, prosecuting a case you will be defending." She shook her head, her voice lowering to a husky whisper. "If you hadn't backed off . . ."

Horrified at the extent of her confession, Laura looked away in embarrassment. What had been to her an awakening experience had probably been to him merely a matter of routine. He must indeed think her a babe in the woods!

Nervously fingering a monogrammed letter opener, she steeled herself for a taunt that never came. Rather, she felt a strong finger beneath her chin, gently turning her face to his. Until that moment, his hand had never even touched her, save the introductory hand-shake he'd given her that morning in court.

"You must be one of the most forthright women I've met." She could only guess at the flicker of admiration in his eyes, it came and went so quickly, to be replaced by a more mischievous twinkle, as his hand fell away. "I'll see you soon."

So abrupt was his change of mood, veering from the earnest to the playful in an instant, that Laura was left with a frown of disbelief on her face, long after he had left the room.

23

Two

Maxwell Kraig had been right. He was to see her soon, much sooner than Laura had anticipated and in a setting which was to greatly tax her willpower.

The fundraiser for Franklin Potter had been on the schedule for months. Hundreds of supporters from his own Hampshire County, as well as friends and associates from farther reaches of the state, had each paid a hefty sum for the privilege of sharing an evening with the renowned district attorney, all proceeds earmarked for the chief prosecutor's anticipated reelection bid the following year.

Laura had taken extra care in dressing for the sake of her father, who had flown in from Chicago for the fundraiser and, more importantly, to spend the weekend with his youngest child, and only daughter.

Now as they entered the crowded hall, the pride on her father's face justified her painstaking preparations. Her pink silk dress was of cocktail length and belted, its gently flowing skirt mirroring the soft fullness of its long sleeves, a plunging neckline the only concession to the woman-as-temptress look that Laura dared to make. She wore delicate silver sandals, high-heeled as always, her slim legs moving gracefully as she walked. Her black hair hung to her shoulders, its side strands drawn up and back, secured with a tiny silk rose on one side, matching her dress, the vividness of its color and the darkness of her hair a perfect foil for the alabaster sheen of her skin. The only jewelry she wore were the exquisite pearl studs at her ears, though the burgundy shine on her fingertips glistened as richly as a handful of rubies.

"Life as a lawyer must be agreeing with you, sweetheart," her father quipped, squeezing her affectionately about the waist. "You look marvelous!" Hand in hand, they proceeded to the bar.

"You're looking pretty dapper, yourself," Laura whispered fondly. Her father had reached his late fifties with a headful of dark hair, graying only slightly now at the temples to give him an even more distinguished look than his proud carriage and impeccable costume conveyed. Although Laura had taken her slimness and her skin coloring from her mother, in all other respects she was her father's daughter. The mane of thick, straight hair, the blueness of the eyes, the independence of spirit—Laura and Howard Grandine were of the same mold.

Typical of the political function, handshaking and backslapping were the rule as the pair wandered casually through the crowd. Though Howard Grandine's practice was located primarily in the Midwest, his ring of friends spanned the country.

Laura always enjoyed being with him socially, as she had done so often after her mother died, filling in as his escort at dinners and parties, business functions and fundraisers. Her father handled himself well, and she had learned much from him. Now her training justified itself as she graciously acknowledged introduction after introduction, expertly making many herself as familiar faces passed or stopped. It was the same "Howard, how are you?" and the "Good to see you, Mr. Grandine," or the "Laura, we hear good things about you," to which she had grown accustomed.

"Sandy!" she called, catching sight of her favorite trooper several bodies away. "Sandy!"

It took a moment for him to locate the source of the voice, but Sandy was soon at her side. "You look gorgeous, Laura!" He placed a brotherly peck on her cheek before catching sight of her partner. "Mr. Grandine," he introduced himself, "I'm Sandy Chatfield. How are you, sir?"

"Not bad at all, thank you," the other responded, with a vigorous handshake and a warm smile. "So this"—he directed his question to Laura out of the corner of his mouth—"is the fellow who so ably assists my little girl?" Three years before, Laura might have bristled at her father's reference. Now, however, her own self-esteem was such that she merely grinned indulgently and let her father flex his muscle.

"Yes, sir," Sandy replied enthusiastically, "and I might add that I can't remember having had a more pleasant assignment in years." Laura had to laugh at the last; Sandy was only in his mid-thirties, yet he often spoke like a long-time veteran.

"Aw, Sandy," she teased, "you must say that to all the girls you work with." The two exchanged meaningful glances, then laughed at the joke; Laura was the only female any trooper had been assigned to in years, and they both knew it.

"Am I interrupting anything confidential?" That velvet tone which Laura recognized immediately broke through the laughter, sobering Sandy instantly, Laura soon after. Neither the former, with his self-proclaimed hawk-eyes, nor the latter, with the sixth sense that had been in operation that other afternoon, had been aware of his attendance at the fundraiser, yet here he stood, all six foot three of him, looking more handsome than ever in his dark suit, cream-colored shirt, and muted paisley print tie. At his elbow was an elegant woman, slim and auburn-haired, sophistication swirling about her chiffon-gowned figure.

To Laura's even greater surprise, it was her father who came to her own tongue-tied rescue. "Max! How are you?" he exclaimed, reaching across to capture the hand that the other had already extended.

"Just fine, Howard! What are *you* doing all the way out here?" There was surprise in Max's greeting, the slightest slant of confusion on his brow.

Howard Grandine's eyes twinkled mischievously in anticipation of some fun. "Same thing you are, no doubt!" he answered noncommittally. Gradually recovering from the appearance of Maxwell Kraig, Laura had begun to sense her father's amusement . . . and to surmise its cause. Silently, she stood and watched, waiting to see exactly how perceptive Max could be.

"I've known Frank for a good many years," Max explained, "and, as it is, I have other business at this end of the state." His gaze suddenly shifted to Laura. A suggestion of a frown creased his brow as he looked back at Howard, then settled his brown eyes on Laura once more. In that instant she knew the ruse was up. Proof

27

followed. "If I'd known that Laura was *your* daughter, Howard, I might have refused to take the case. The Grandine mind is legendary in legal circles."

"You would never have turned down the case," Laura contradicted him lightly, "for a reason like that." Then she turned hastily to her father. "I didn't realize that you and Max were acquainted." She tempered the accusation of her words with a mother-scolding-child tone of voice.

It was Max who explained, a relaxed smile playing over his features as his eyes played over hers. "Howard and I have worked together. He has given invaluable counsel to my clients on any number of instances. We refer each other cases regularly."

A perceptible squeeze to his arm by his noticeably impatient date brought Max's attention away from Laura. "But, excuse me," he apologized quickly, "may I introduce Marilyn Hough." He made the introductions all around, he and Sandy exchanging stilted nods.

"Maxwell"—the woman's voice sounded clearly seductive and totally out of place—"Alex is waiting. We were to meet him five minutes ago." Checking his watch, Max nodded, though a suggestion of annoyance hovered at the back of his eyes.

"Howard, you'll have to excuse us. Will you be staying for dinner?"

Howard Grandine laughed heartily. "At the price we paid for these tickets, you bet I'll be staying for dinner. Besides, it may take me several hours to locate Frank in this crowd . . . and he *is* the major reason I'm here!"

Laura was caught off-guard when Max

28

nonchalantly suggested they meet at the buffet table in an hour. Howard accepted the invitation before she could draw a breath in protest. Dinner was the last thing she wanted to have in the presence of this man. He was dangerous enough to work with, but, after hours, she sensed he could devastate her!

"Why did you commit us to having dinner with him?" she whispered as soon as Max and his date had moved on. Sandy shared her sentiment, a scowl having settled on his previously gentle features.

"I enjoy the man, sweetheart. Besides, now that I find he's here, there is a matter I'd like to discuss with him. You may well find it interesting." There was a hint of censure in his tone, which quickly softened to curiosity. "Does the prospect of being with him distress you, Laura?"

A pinkness akin to that of her dress crept up from her neck. Annoyed with herself for the sensitivity, Laura willed the color into abeyance as she feigned an air of indifference. "It doesn't distress me, exactly, but we will be on opposite sides of the courtroom when the Stallway case comes to trial. I'm not sure it's wise to . . . be with him."

"To the contrary," her father corrected gently, "it is possible that during our discussion tonight, you may get a preview of the lawyer at work in the man's mind." Laura saw the truth of his reasoning.

"I suppose you're right," she admitted begrudgingly. "Just keep him away from me!" As soon as the words were out, she regretted them. It was a suspicious expression that father showered on daughter this time around.

"I don't think you'll have much to worry

29

about," he began cautiously. "He has a date who seemed to have little patience for the attention he gave you just now." Laura glanced away in a moment of petulance. If anything, her father's comment should have eased her worries. She certainly would be safer from Max's magnetism if his date were present. Yet, that very presence disturbed her.

Standing unobtrusively by, Sandy now paralleled her own thoughts. "She was a beauty, that dame," he whistled under his breath, his words taking on the more crude intonation which he could adopt or discard at will.

Impulsively, Laura whirled about. "She was a beauty, all right—if you like them with their nose in the air and their brain in their pinkie . . ." Crossly, she looked off into the crowd, missing the questioning gaze that passed between Sandy and her father.

"Come on, sweetheart." It was her father who came to her aid. "I think I see Thad Barstow. He'd love to see you after all these years." Guiding her gently, Howard Grandine left the police officer to his own musings, as father and daughter moved away. By the time they reached their destination, Laura had regained her good humor sufficiently to play the poised and charming daughter of old.

The poise remained intact during the next hour, as once again she immersed herself in the enjoyment of seeing old friends and meeting new ones. With a legal career of her own, she found herself particularly at ease and, indeed, in demand. Sadly, she mused, people seemed to value most what was reported in the newspapers. Even some of the most trivial cases she'd prosecuted had been given coverage by the local press; now people begged to hear little tidbits about one case or the other. Well used to parrying requests without compromising her own position, Laura was in her element.

The buffet table had been newly replenished by the time they reached it. Cautiously glancing around, Laura saw no sign of Max Kraig.

"Well, it looks like we've been stood up." She breathed exultantly. "Let's get some food. I've had enough to drink on an empty stomach to keep me on the ceiling for a week."

"That's an interesting prospect." Even before she turned around, the quivering of her insides announced the arrival of her nemesis.

"Max!" Her father welcomed him. "We were beginning to wonder whether you'd make it back after all."

Max's dark eyes grew even more so as they focussed on Laura. "For an opportunity to spend time with such a delightful family, I'd risk life and limb."

Laura was faintly aware of a hand at the back of her waist, warm and supportive. It took several moments for her to realize that it did not belong to her father. "Won't Marilyn be joining us?" she inquired politely, with a calmness deceptive of the inner turmoil the man's appearance had instantly generated.

"She wanted to spend some time with a friend. I didn't think you would miss her." There was a devilish glint in his eye that took the implication a step further than his words had.

Laura parried the suggestion artfully, leaning slightly nearer and injecting an intimate, though mocking, note in her voice. "But *you* may miss

31

her. There's not much other action of that type around."

Howard made his presence felt with a good-natured grunt. "*I* may be the one who misses her, if you two don't come get some dinner."

Conversation was held at a minimum as they passed down the length of the buffet, helping themselves to lobster and crabmeat salads, ham slices, sweet-and-sour salmon, and other dishes. Much to Laura's consternation, her father led them to a small table in a relatively secluded corner. Once seated, Laura scanned the buffet table for a sign of Sandy.

Max read her mind. "If it's that bodyguard you're looking for, I assured him that your father would protect you."

Laura's head twirled about, a glower at the ready, until she caught the warm, even enchanting touch of humor on Max's face. Unable to help herself, her resistance melted instantly. And, yes, her father was here. He would be a perfect buffer, should the need arise.

From the start Laura's fears were unfounded. Howard and Max did indeed have a legal matter to discuss. As her father had promised, Laura was fascinated, as much by the subject as by the quickness of Max's mind and his ability to sift out the essence of a problem and hone in on it. With begrudging admiration, she noted the wealth of reference cases he had filed cerebrally, to be called forth at will. Her father had been right; she did gain valuable insight into the way the man operated. And it might just help her in planning her own case, she mused, as she poked absently at her food.

By the time they finished eating, coffee had

been brought to the table, hot and strong, just as Laura liked it. Howard grinned jovially. "I have this strange feeling that neither of you will be wanting any dessert," he announced, as he patted his own slightly too snug vest, "but I for one wouldn't miss it. I also see an old sweetheart of mine." His eye twinkled naughtily. "So"—he glanced at Max briefly before his gaze settled on his disconcerted daughter—"if you'll excuse me . . ." Despite his famous I-know-you-can-do-it-sweetheart look, Laura felt abandoned. And furious! How could her father have left her alone with this man? Now as she watched him saunter off, she wondered at her own timidity. She wasn't really frightened of Max, but rather of the power which he seemed to wield over the world in general, over her in particular.

"A penny for your thoughts?" Laura's heart lurched at the deeply melodious tone that floated the short distance from where Max sat, leaning back, studying her intently.

Darting a final glance at her father's retreating figure, she improvised. "I was . . . thinking how wonderful it is to see my dad again." Whether the faint flush on her cheeks gave her away, she couldn't tell. For a moment she feared he would call her on it; his eye bore such a disbelieving glint. Then to her relief, he allowed her the face-saving gesture.

"He's quite a man . . . and quite a lawyer."

"Yes." She smiled proudly now. "He is well known and respected."

"From what I see," Max said thoughtfully, "Grandine, Harper, and Boyd is one of the finest corporate firms in the Midwest. And since Howard is the senior partner, having built the

33

firm from scratch, he deserves most of the credit."

Laura nodded her head in recognition of the compliment. "You *have* done your homework, haven't you?"

The added element of warmth that flared in his gaze prepared Laura for a slight redirection of the discussion. "Yes, but sometimes I miss things. For example, had I known that Howard Grandine had such a beautiful daughter stashed away in the Windy City, I would have made a point to meet with him personally rather than conducting business over the telephone."

"But I haven't been stashed away, as you put it, in Chicago," she protested.

"Ah, yes," he agreed, emphasizing each word. "Another error of mine. You certainly are not the smalltown girl I had originally supposed."

Laura laughed. "Now, what ever gave you that idea?"

Max's eyes narrowed. "I seem to recall some line about sophisticated luxury versions, one of which you claimed not to be. Yet, for Howard Grandine's daughter not to be considered as such is hard to swallow.

You certainly made as elegant an entrance as any woman tonight." The heat of his gaze brought heightened color to her cheeks. "But that blush seems to keep popping up. It's a very innocent touch. Perhaps we have two different women here, in one very beautiful body." Laura fumed silently at her inability to come up with a suitable rejoinder. "But now I've made it worse," her tormentor went on with mock regret. "Just tell me one last thing." He clearly enjoyed her discomfort. "Do you blush in court?"

"No!" On professional ground, there was no equivocating.

"Now that's a relief," the low voice taunted gently. "The blush has a definite debilitating effect on me."

"Then I may just try it one day," she proposed defensively. "It could be amusing." He had set himself up for that one, and she knew it. Pleasure was forthcoming, nevertheless, as a broad smile spanned his masculine features, spreading a happiness in its wake that included Laura within its sphere.

"Tell me," he asked, still smiling, though his gaze had grown more pensive. "Did you go into law because of your father?"

Laura thought for a moment, sipping her coffee before she spoke. "If you're asking whether my father pressured me, the answer is no. On the other hand, I can't deny that his being a lawyer, and the subsequent exposure to the law I received, did influence my decision."

"Is it just you and your dad?"

"No. I have an older brother. Unfortunately, I don't see Jack very often."

"Where does he live?" The questions flowed freely, yet, to Laura's pleasure, there was a genuine interest behind them.

"Washington. He's the black sheep of the family!" She chuckled at the in-family joke, then, in response to Max's curiosity, she explained. "He works for the government as a linguist. He's fluent in seven languages."

Max's grin stole several beats from her heart. "That's quite a black sheep! Would you believe that I'm considered the black sheep of *my* family?"

"You're kidding!" Laura's gaze narrowed dubiously.

"Nope." He shook his dark head, a thatch of hair lowering onto his forehead. Fighting the uncanny impulse to comb it back with her fingers, she clutched at her coffee cup. "For generations my family has worked exclusively in the family business. We manufacture paper products," he explained, his face taking on a soft, faraway look.

"You said you were born in New York. Is that where your family lives?"

He hesitated. In that instant, Laura wondered whether he regretted opening up to her. It was a victory when he spoke, apparently resolving any qualms in her favor.

"Yes. They live, for the most part, in Westchester—my parents, two brothers and a sister, and their assorted families."

"What are their reactions to your work?" Again Laura saw an unsureness cloud his gaze. This time, however, he was merely seeking the best way to express his answer.

"You have to understand," he began, his brown eyes fixed intensively on her own glittering blue, "that they did not wish me to become a lawyer." He went on quickly, nipping Laura's perplexity in the bud. "Lawyers were traditionally employees in the family business, rather than family itself."

"But the type of law you practice is a world away from that!"

"You know that and I know that," he sighed, "but my family saw it differently for quite some time."

"And now?" Her eyebrows lifted expectantly.

Max smiled in that relaxed, self-assured way

that made his words superfluous. "Now they know it too. It's taken a long time, but they have come around. At least that was the impression I got when my father asked me to autograph his copy of *Eleventh-Street Defense*," he added playfully. Something in his tone suggested the ability to keep his own success well within perspective. Laura liked that; and, to her subsequent chagrin, she told him so.

"It's refreshing to find someone who is not so hung up on his own ego that he can't laugh at himself." The flames that flared in Max's eyes suddenly took on that more dangerous context that Laura found so disturbing.

"Go out with me tomorrow night, Laura?" He hadn't laid a finger on her, yet those compelling eyes hooked her once again. One part of her would have welcomed a continuation of discussions similar to those they'd begun on this evening, but her answer had to remain the same. Wordlessly, she shook her head.

Then, far from the devastating attempts at persuasion she had expected, she found her hand grasped quickly and firmly. "Then at least dance with me once tonight." It was a statement, rather than an invitation, and before Laura had a chance to demur, she was drawn out of her seat and into step alongside Max. His hand was warm and strong about hers, a delightful sensation, had her pride not been faintly bruised by his bold behavior.

"And if I refuse?" She tested him, raising her voice as they approached the ever-growing crescendo of music in the crowded ballroom.

He stopped abruptly and looked her daringly in the eye. "Then I'll pick you up and carry you, screaming and yelling, if need be, to the center of the dance floor. And you wouldn't like that very much, would you, Madame Prosecutor? Wouldn't do much for your image, hmm?" He teased, half-playful, half-warning. Reading the acquiescence in her eyes while ignoring the anger lurking in their depths, he resumed his course until they arrived in a relatively less-congested area, where he swung her gently around into the circle of his arms. Any anger which had loomed moments earlier vanished in that first instant as he deftly brought her willowy frame into contact with his long, firm one, one hand clasping hers against his lapel, the other guiding her protectively, its weight feather light but ever felt as it roamed her back. In perfect syncopation they rocked easily in time to the slow tune. A versatile dancer, Laura secretly preferred the closeness of this more traditional dance, where both partners could exalt in each other as well as in the music. And in this particular situation, she did exalt in her partner, as together they enjoyed the gentle beat.

Her body melted against his, her free hand creeping recklessly to his neck, where her fingers rested in his hair. Her head nestled comfortably at his collar-bone, his chin caressing the soft tendrils of hair at her temple. The closeness was a drug, lulling her toward divine euphoria. Eyes closed, she followed his lead, her legs moving responsively to his, aware of the hardness of his thigh, the strength of his torso, the breadth of the chest against which she had so happily dissolved.

Echoing her thoughts, Max uttered a faintly sensuous "Mmmmm," before wrapping her even more tightly in his embrace and whirling her around in a spurt of movement, then settling once more to the hypnotic pace of the dance. Laura was aware of the touch of his lips against her forehead, a delicious sensation she had no wish to disturb.

She was conscious of the clean, masculine smell that had embedded itself on her memory and became one more item on the growing list of enticements the man held. Her hand was released to rest against his chest, allowing him the freedom of both hands to sensuously mold her body to the contours of his. From deep within Laura realized a sense of fulfillment at the closeness, though her mind was too befuddled by it to ponder either its cause or its meaning.

The final chords of the music came as a disturbing jolt, bringing Laura reluctantly back to the world of reason. When she would have stepped from the supporting warmth of Max's body, however, she found herself within a steel-banded prison, held at his whim. She tilted her head back and looked into the eyes which gazed so softly down at her. Neither of them had spoken since they had taken to the dance floor. There had been a higher form of communication in use, making words unnecessary. Both knew this, as they continued to gaze at one another.

"You're a very dangerous man, Maxwell Kraig," she finally said, more breathlessly than she had expected.

"Would you care to elaborate on that?" he challenged softly, his breath fanning her face intimately.

Impishly, she shook her head. "No way. I . . . think that I'd better find my father now." It was the last thing she wanted to do, the first thing being to stay in the delightfully heady haven that Max had built for her. Yet she was, indeed, on dangerous ground. Unfortunately, though, she needed Max's permission to leave, so strongly did his arms hold her. And he had something else in mind.

"Come here," he ordered, raising one arm up to span the curve of her shoulders as he turned to walk beside her to a far corner. The lights had begun to flicker wildly as the band launched into a hearty disco beat.

"Where are you taking me?" she yelled above the outpouring of sound, the uproar behind them masking the trepidation in her voice.

Max lowered his dark head to her ear. "I want to show you something." They had reached a wide column, one of four in each of the corners of the room. Before she realized what was happening, Laura found herself backed against its dark side, the world obliterated from her view by the tall hulk of the man in front of her.

"Max—" Her words of protest were stilled by his mouth, swooping down to capture hers with infinite precision. She resisted at first, squirming to extricate herself, only to find his body more fully against hers, imprisoning her in a web of growing arousal. The hands which had briefly pushed against his chest now splayed across it, crushed against him, yet tingling with the contact.

Hungrily, his lips devoured hers, stoking her own appetite until her response was as demanding. If later she was dismayed by the magnitude of her own need, her only consolation was in the knowledge that his was as great. For now, however, her only thought was of the new and exciting feelings, somehow less frightening

40

than they had once been, that the man evoked in her.

With a ragged moan he pulled her away from the column to wind his arms around her slimness. She gasped helplessly as his fingertips brushed her breasts, then ran one hand over his shoulder to weave its fingers into the hair at his nape, subconsciously giving him even greater access to that most sensitive breast.

Suddenly, he drew his head back to look into her eyes. The smoldering flame she saw in his startled her into the awareness of where they were and . . . who they were. Sensing her thoughts, he released her slowly, taking a deep and unsteady breath as he did so. As relieved as Laura was, something within her cried at the sudden loss.

"You are a very dangerous woman, Laura Grandine," Max crooned huskily, as his gaze continued to hold hers.

She struggled to regain her balance. "Was that what you wanted to show me?" she mocked. Her tremulous whisper took all sarcasm from her words.

One side of his mouth quirked fiendishly. "Among other things." Laura did not have to ask about those other things. She had felt them all too clearly and knew that she would spend long hours remembering them . . . and trying not to remember them.

"I'd really better get back." She tried again, not trusting herself to withstand much more of his charm. Perhaps, she mused, he was right. There was something dangerous within her, something which Maxwell Kraig had been the only man ever to unleash. She had, over the years,

41

had her share of male company and manly kisses. Yet never before had she been affected like this.

Lightly fingering a loose tendril of hair by her cheek, Max looked at her lips, still warm and moist from his kiss. "You're right. Daddy will be looking for his little girl and . . . I do have a date around here somewhere." It was an exaggerated sigh that mocked her, his taunt arousing a sudden and petulant fury in her.

"If that's the way you treat your dates, remind me never to be one," she fumed, whirling around to escape. An iron grip on her wrist stayed her. With deliberate slowness she turned her head, first to his hand, then to his face, willing a fire in her gaze to underscore her irritation and demand an explanation for his hold on her. She was not prepared for the hoarseness in his otherwise good-humored tone.

"Dammit, if you aren't as sexy when you're angry!"

Incensed further she clenched both fists and teeth. "Sorry, but Daddy's waiting." She mocked his words, tugging to free her hand from his steel grip.

"Then I'll take my leave. Good night, Laura." He spoke softly, only the barest hint of humor now in his gaze as he placed a light kiss on her cheek, released her wrist, and walked smoothly off, leaving Laura to seethe.

Remaining in the shadows, she sought the support of that same broad column to still her quaking limbs. Then with every ounce of clear-headedness she could muster, she attempted to make some sense out of what had taken place. Unfortunately, she saw things all too clearly. For what emerged, above all, was not so much the audacity of the man, but rather the nature of her own reaction to it. She was annoyed. Her pride had been injured. She felt strangely hurt. Disappointment had followed the termination of his kiss. Frustration had overblown his patronizing comment. Envy had soared on his reminder of the silky sophisticate awaiting him.

All too clearly Laura recognized these emotions. Not quite so clearly did she know what to do about them. Suddenly she'd had enough of the party. Straightening her shoulders and raising her chin, she left her shelter and made her way around the dancing populace, then back through the crowd to where she finally located her father, engaged in conversation with the esteemed district attorney for whom the entire evening's bash had been orchestrated.

"Ah-hah!" she exclaimed, winding her arm through her father's. "I've killed two birds with one stone." Her wary eye in his direction gave Franklin Potter warning of her intent.

It was her father whose attempt to cajole her backfired. "Why, Laura! I thought you'd be busy dancing—"

"I'll bet you did." She chided him, though her irritation was rapidly falling victim to the comforting familiarity of the two men before her. Lest it fade into oblivion, she turned to Frank, impaling him with her most stern expression. "You and I have something to discuss."

"Laura!" Again it was her father. "That's no way to talk to the star of the party!"

Frank, however, was more than able to handle the hard-biting temper of the young woman he'd known since she'd been a child. "Monday morning, ten o'clock. How's that?"

43

"But, Frank—" she began, reluctant to be put off when she knew that much of her fire would have burned out by then.

"Monday, Laura." It was the D.A. at his most final. Laura quickly shut her mouth.

It had perhaps been a good thing that Frank had refused to discuss Maxwell Kraig that evening. Not only would it have been inappropriate, given the setting, but Laura's own thoughts were still too raw.

After spending most of the weekend with her father, then seeing him back off to Chicago Sunday afternoon, she had put things into perspective. The only thing she had to discuss with Frank was how to handle Maxwell Kraig on the legal level. Anything else was her own personal affair.

"Okay, let's have it." Frank broached the topic as soon as Laura had been seated in his office. She held a cup of fresh coffee, snatched from the percolator that was earmarked for the small crowd that passed through that door in the course of the day.

"Tell me everything you know about him, Frank." She paused at the studied innocence on his face. "And don't tell me you don't know about whom I am talking!"

"He has quite an effect on you, doesn't he?" There was humor, verging on enjoyment, as the perceptive D.A. confronted her.

"You think this is pretty funny, don't you?" she accused pertly.

The man with the round red cheeks and thinning gray hair grinned. "It's just that you're usually so unflappable, Laura. You're too serious sometimes. I enjoy seeing you flustered, for a change."

"Well, thank you," she snapped with an indignant look. "I sometimes wonder whether, between you and my father, you'd rather see me married and raising children. You're both rushing me, Frank," she warned gently.

The politician lowered his head, looking at her now over his wire-rimmed spectacles. "You know you're one of the best lawyers I've had in years. I'd be in rough straits without you! But you do take things too seriously sometimes."

The slim hand held up before her signaled for his silence. "I think, Mr. District Attorney, that we've gotten off the subject. I want to know everything about Max Kraig. Please, Frank, whatever you tell me will help me in planning my case and its strategy." She had practiced the line repeatedly; when it came out, she did feel convinced that her interest was purely professional.

Apparently in agreement with her reasoning, Frank began. "I've known Max for six, seven years now. He's a tough lawyer, Laura. And a good one. He's honest and hard-working."

"Sounds ominous," she quipped, sipping her coffee as the D.A. continued.

"You should remember three things about him, Laura." He leaned back in his seat, letting a hand rest on the cushion of his generous middle. "First of all, don't let the media image lull you into thinking that he rides along on reputation alone. He doesn't! Max is a consummate lawyer. He is well prepared and shrewd. Nothing slips by him." Laura could have already told him that!

"Second," he went on systematically, "he is an expert in psyching out both witnesses and

45

jurors. He knows just when to charm them and just when to stick the knife in. He can be the master of understatement when it suits him." Laura swallowed convulsively; he seemed to be the master of far too many things.

"I wish I had *half* his skill in the courtroom," he added with a sigh of admiration.

"And I'm sure," Laura interjected diplomatically, "that he wishes he had *half* your skill as a politician. Everything is relative, Frank! Now"— she paused to get the D.A.'s full attention—"how about that third thing I should remember?"

He grinned wickedly. "Please remember"— his voice was lower than usual—"that he has a devastating effect on women."

For a moment Laura's sentiments came sharply close to the surface. "Now what is that supposed to mean?" If it was a personal warning he wished to issue, he was too late. Frank's obvious disapproval of her assumption immediately brought a flush to Laura's cheeks. She had misinterpreted him, taking his words personally when they had been intended on a purely legal level. "Oh, you mean, jury type of thing," she mumbled apologetically.

"Precisely." He overlooked her lapse. "Female witnesses are apt to be awed, perhaps intimidated by him. That we cannot help. But the jury is another matter. He's bound to charm the pants— figuratively, of course—off any female juror."

Laura's own legal acuity grasped this dilemma. "I'm in a bind. On the one hand, considering that the victim was a lovely, young coed at Smith, those women on the jury would be highly sympathetic to the prosecution. Max Kraig, however, can turn that all around, just with his damned sex appeal . . ." She stood up, dropping her empty foam cup into the wastebasket as she walked to the window. Despite the snow that had both fallen and been shoveled against the basement-level window, Frank's office still held a charming dog's-eye view of the main street which dissected Northampton.

"Laura"—the D.A.'s softer tone brought her head around with a start—"don't let him snow you." It was a personal warning, after all. Even sensing its futility, she gave lip service to her credo.

"I can handle it, Frank." Her voice was calm, her gaze steady. Only her insides swirled in testimony to her doubts. "I see Max as a lawyer, a professional. We are on opposite sides of the courtroom. You know how much my work means to me, and this case . . ."

He picked up where she left off. "This case will mean big things for you. You've earned it, Laura. In the three years you've been in my office, you've done your share of assault and batteries, larcenies, breaking and enterings. That job you did prosecuting the Coolidge Inn armed robbery last summer clinched it. You're ready. This is your case. But—" He hesitated. Not very often was Frank Potter at a loss for words; this seemed to be one of those rare times. Laura waited patiently, if a bit apprehensively.

"But," he finally resumed, "I do worry about you, personally, Laura. You know how I feel about Howard. You could be my own daughter— and I'd warn *her* about Max Kraig."

Laura came around to the front of his desk. "Is he that horrible?" Her voice held a mildly ludicrous note.

A shrug of unsureness bounced over the D.A.'s shoulders. "I like the man personally. But he does seem to give an image of moving very quickly, both to and from the prettiest girls around. He has never married. Strange"—he lowered his voice—"he has so much to give, yet seems to have no desire for a wife, children . . ." Laura conjured up a vivid image of Phyllis Potter, Frank's faithful, if invisible, wife, and their family of eight mostly grown children. Poor Frank, she mused; he would have trouble understanding.

"Maybe he's just . . . not ready," she suggested as dispassionately as she could.

The D.A. looked keenly at her. "He's thirty-nine, Laura. I'd say it's time. But, acch," he reproached himself, "it's none of my business what he does with his life. But you . . . that *is* my business. I don't want you hurt." There was a vehemence in his tone which touched her. In a spontaneous gesture she walked around the desk and put an arm around his shoulders.

"I know that, and you have no idea how much I value it. I won't be hurt. Please believe me, Frank—this is just another case with just another lawyer." She squeezed his shoulders as a final note, yet her own words returned to haunt her in the next few days.

Just another lawyer. Just another lawyer. If that was the case, why was she plagued by memories of him—his dark face, his large hands, his powerful arms, his mind-drugging kiss?

Three

By the middle of the week Laura congratulated herself on having regained control of the situation. It was simply a matter of more deeply immersing herself in her work. There were court appearances to be made, cases to be researched, tactics to be chosen. Having pushed herself even harder than usual, she was, by Friday, tired and the slightest bit more touchy than normal.

The morning had been spent with the state troopers, trying to ferret out the admissible evidence on an armed robbery case she would be prosecuting. Having hurriedly picked up a yogurt and coffee at the small cafeteria across the street, she returned to her office to review the results of that morning's meeting.

As fate would have it, the telephone began to ring. And ring. One call after another came through, each concerning entirely different matters, none concerning the one case on which her mind had been focussed. Then, forty-five minutes later, Sandy walked innocently into her office to give her the news she least needed.

"Courthouse grapevine has it that Maxwell Kraig is visiting his client at the county jail," he announced tartly, his eyes sticking to Laura's for instant analysis of her reaction.

Her voice shot up in surprise. "He's here? In Northampton? Now?"

He nodded. "So says the grapevine." Then

49

his eyes widened as Laura dramatically slammed shut the book with which she'd been tussling.

"That does it!" she declared loudly. "I'm getting out of here. Between that telephone and . . . other interruptions, I won't get a thing done."

Sandy was bewildered. "Hey, Laura. It's no big thing. Is he supposed to show up here too?"

"Not that I know of. But I'm not taking any chances." She piled several pads of paper atop the book, added several pens, and was busily putting folders into her briefcase as she spoke. "I have too much work to get done to risk an afternoon of interruptions!"

Both hands on his hips, he confronted her. "And where are you going?"

"Upstairs to the library. But"—she leveled her gaze and raised a pointing finger at him—"you are not to tell a soul. Got that?"

Suddenly, he burst into a sly grin. "You're trying to avoid him, aren't you?"

"Avoid who?"

"Laura, don't pull that one on me again. Kraig. Are you trying to avoid him?"

Exasperated, she mirrored his stance, putting both hands boldly on her waist, and sent him a grimace. "Of course not! But I don't want his interruption any more than I do . . . yours, Sandy, old pal!" Her face softened at the end. Even had it not, the seasoned trooper would not have taken her spiked words to heart. He knew her too well.

"Okay," he acquiesced, turning to the door with a smile. "It's your loss." Then, abruptly, he faced her once more. "But I agree with you about Kraig."

Laura frowned. "What do you agree with?"

"I don't think you should see him. Frankly, I

50

don't like the man. And I wouldn't trust him further than a—"

"Tsk, tsk, Sandy, that's just your natural prejudice. I *do* trust him. But there's no reason why I have to see him today. If he wants something, he can make an appointment, like everyone else!"

Sandy held the door as she walked past him into the hall, her arms laden now with the tools of her trade, plus the heavy wool reefer and scarf she had pulled off a hanger on her way. As he came alongside her, he nodded his approval. "Spoken like a truly hard-nosed prosecutor! Say, can I give you a hand?"

Shifting the weight of her book more comfortably she shook her head. "No, thanks. But you can give Sara the message at the switchboard that I'll be incommunicado for the afternoon." She lowered her voice to sound purposefully mysterious, yet her gaze warned Sandy to say no more. With two fingers to his lips, he indicated they were sealed, then left her to maneuver the stairs herself.

Her good humor returned slowly as she settled herself in the second-floor library. It was a favorite spot of hers, containing cushioned leather chairs, a long oak table, and floor-to-ceiling bookshelves lined with a prime selection of legal reference books and journals. There was a certain pacifying effect here. More often than not, it was deserted, as it was now. She loved its silence, its warm ancient-lamp lighting, its distinctly musty smell.

Quickly she became engrossed in her reading and notetaking, the passage of time holding no import as she had no further call to return to her office. She had worked for an hour or two when she decided to check a cross-reference on a case.

She climbed up the sturdy ladder standing before the shelves and withdrew the volume she wanted from one of the higher shelves. She remained in a half-seated position with her back to the door and scanned its contents, quickly locating and verifying the information she sought. She turned once again on the ladder, to replace the book in its slot, then reversed direction. With a loud gasp of surprise, she realized that she was not alone.

"You frightened me!" she exclaimed breathlessly, clutching at the ladder with one hand, her chest with the other. "Do you always creep up on people like that?" Her embarrassment took the form of annoyance and was directed at Maxwell Kraig, who stood in all his masculine glory by the foot of the ladder.

He cast a nonchalant glance at the worn carpet as he spoke. "I am sorry. Had I realized that the carpet would absorb the sound of my footsteps, I would have put bells on my toes." His blatant attempt at humor did nothing to put Laura at ease.

"You could have . . . spoken . . . or s-something," she stammered. "And did you have to come right up so close?" In a quandary as to how to most gracefully descend the ladder now, she continued to babble.

"Actually"—Max's low tone was as smooth as she remembered it—"I've been standing by the door watching since you climbed up there. I thought I could give you a hand coming down."

"I don't—" Her words of denial were cut short as his strong hands circled her waist and effortlessly lifted her down, lingering a moment too long in their hold for her psychological comfort before they released her completely and disappeared into his trouser pockets. It was proving to be a favorite stance of his, a maddening one for Laura, emphasizing as it did the force of his thighs and the slimness of his hips.

"Thank you," she mumbled softly as she returned to her seat and dissolved into it, outwardly assuming that Max had come to do some spot research of his own, though suspecting he had not. A shot out of the corner of her eye located his topcoat and briefcase by the door; he made no move to retrieve them. Rather, he eased his rangy frame into the chair opposite hers at the table, and waited. As the minutes passed, he made neither sound nor movement.

Productive work was out of the question. Worse than that, the situation was ludicrous. In fact the more Laura thought of dark, compelling Max sitting there, as quiet as a mouse, doing absolutely nothing but studying the top of her silky hair, the more irresistible he became.

Finally, with a smirk of helplessness, she put down her pen and looked up into the face that innocently beamed back at her. "You're impossible, do you know that?"

He raised an eyebrow. "Impossible? I might have hoped for delightful, charming, witty, or even irresistible. Must I settle for impossible?"

"Yes," she declared vehemently, fearing that he was indeed all of the others, though adamant that his ego be spared further enlargement.

He shrugged his shoulders in mock resignation. "Then impossible it is. How have you been, Laura?"

She had been just fine until he showed up. Now her pulse raced strangely. "Very busy," she hedged.

53

"What are you working on?" His eyes fell to the papers before her.

"I'm trying to prepare for an armed robbery. We need to use a piece of evidence that could be fairly controversial. I'm trying to find legal precedence."

"May I see your notes?" In his more business-like form Laura felt more relaxed.

"Help yourself," she offered, pushing the papers toward him. She was not one to let pride refuse an offer of assistance, even one from the opposition.

Actually, his gesture had a side benefit which Laura had not anticipated. For the few moments that he perused her case summary and notes, she was treated to a free perusal of him. As always she was impressed. His suit was gray with a minute pinstripe running through it, his shirt a very masculine pink, his tie a bolder navy-and-gray. The late afternoon shadow of his beard gave him an even more manly aura, though he already had a monopoly on that dangerous element.

"Try Commonwealth v. Jacobs, 375 Mass.," he suggested, then uncoiled his own length, thumbed across the span of volumes of Massachusetts Reports at the side of the room, and presented her with the one book opened to the page that rapid survey told her held exactly the case she needed.

"That's phenomenal, Max," she exclaimed enthusiastically. "It's perfect. I might have spent two more days trying to locate it. Thanks!" She flashed him her most appreciative smile as she marveled at the man's mind. In addition to everything else, she mused, he had a reference system in his brain, and a memory trained to utilize it to the fullest.

"It's nothing," he murmured softly, then resumed his seat . . . and his silence.

Laura was so intent on wondering what he couldn't do, that it took several moments for her to realize that the two were staring at one another. She forced herself to break the silence.

"You've seen the Stallway boy?"

"Sandy keeps you up-to-date, I see."

Impulsively she began to protest. "Sandy didn't—" Then she stopped, realizing that Sandy had tipped her off. Suddenly her thoughts flew further. "How did you know I was up here. Did Sandy—"

This time Max cut her off, his gaze falling to the creamy expanse of neck and throat visible through the open V of her crepe blouse. "No, Sandy would never betray you. Those troopers have the loyalty of bloodhounds. But I had a feeling you'd be up here. It seemed like . . . your type of place. Do you work here often?"

"Whenever I can," she answered eagerly. "It's always pleasant. And there are rarely interruptions." She threw a pointed look at him, which he chose to let pass.

"Do you have plans for this evening?"

Laura recoiled. Just when she had begun to relax and enjoy his presence, no less his help, he had to spoil things! But she had no intention of hedging on the matter. "No."

"Would you like to have dinner with me?"

It occurred to her that more than anything she would. Yet, she had to stick by her principle. "No."

For the first time Max was impatient with the

response. "Dammit, Laura! Don't you think you're carrying this too far?"

Laura clung stubbornly to her refusal. "We have a working relationship, Max. I've already told you that I made it a practice never to mix—"

"Oh, spare me the lecture," he grumbled, standing up abruptly. "I'd enjoy having dinner with you . . . and so would you. And you know it damned well!" He kept his voice low, but its bridled anger was something new to contend with.

Tongue-tied, Laura merely stared at him. Everything he said was true. She would enjoy having dinner with him. What was she afraid of? Why was she being so rigid? At this point her refusal was merely on principle. Was she right?

When he spoke again, Max's voice was taut and rising rapidly. His eyes flashed, sending a disquieting jolt through her. "You know, you may be beautiful and talented, but you've got about as much common sense as that kid I'm defending! There are times when you sound like a sexless automaton. And I've got better things to do . . ." His voice trailed off as he stalked toward the door, sweeping his coat and briefcase up in one deft motion, then throwing open the door and leaving in a flurry of movement. By the time the door had drifted closed once again, he was gone.

Laura sat in a stupor. Since the moment she had met Max Kraig a week ago, she had experienced a gamut of new, often perplexing emotions. But she had come to respect and like him as a person. Now she had perhaps shattered the good feeling that had existed between them—and the thought of it shattered her.

Suddenly, all pleasure had left the room. An aura of gloom settled over her, thwarting any desire to work. Angry for a wealth of reasons she couldn't begin to sort out, she gathered her things, put on her coat against the January chill, and left the library in nearly as great a huff as Max had.

That evening, as she sat curled in a corner of her sofa, a much-heralded novel open but unheeded in her lap, she brooded. She did want to go out with Maxwell Kraig. He was warm, courteous, intelligent, and handsome. As frightening as was his physical effect on her, she recalled the ecstasy of being held against his strong body, being kissed by his warm lips. That, too, she wanted to experience again.

Saturdays were customarily busy, and this one was, mercifully, no exception. To her dismay, thoughts of Maxwell Kraig managed to intrude in spite of her varied activities. It wasn't enough that the supermarket swallowed up an ever-larger chunk of her weekly pay—and of that pitiful social security check of her landlady, Mrs. Daniels, for whom Laura always did the marketing—but she found herself wondering, as she pushed her basket up one aisle and down the next, what Maxwell Kraig had had for dinner last night, and what she might herself have eaten, had she accepted his invitation.

She imagined, as she jogged the four snow-lined blocks to the YMCA where she taught tennis to "her kids," as they had become known, what Maxwell Kraig did during his spare time to keep in shape. After all, one just didn't look that well and fit by pacing back and forth in front of a jury!

The two friends she met for lunch in a quaint quiche-and-salad place outside the college campus were not much help either. The one thing they wanted to discuss was her career, or, more specifically, the case and the glamorous lawyer defending it.

An afternoon of wading through mid-season discounts on snow gear—boots, parkas, knickers—proved as unhelpful. First she found herself wondering whether Max knew how to cross-country ski—not that it was a relevant issue, since she did not, but she had always wanted to give it a try. Then she had the misfortune of spotting Marilyn Hough, the auburn-haired beauty with whom Max had appeared the weekend before, and she wondered whether Max had sought her company last night after his premature exit from the library. With growing annoyance she imagined his having spent the night at that woman's place, woken up in that woman's bed this morning, shaved and showered in her bathroom—the list of possibilities was infinite.

Laura was jealous! She knew it as clearly as the nose on her face. Yet, what right had she to be, when she had refused two, now three times, to go out with the man? But could she go out with him? How would it affect her performance as a lawyer when she had to face him in court?

No closer to a resolution, she paid for her purchases and began the walk home in the brutally cold wind, drawing her shaggy fur jacket up closer around her. Normally she was vehement about walking. Northampton was a small town; her second-floor apartment was in a two-family house equidistant from the courthouse, the college, the stores, and the Y. Her small Honda was more often than not left in the old garage behind the house. She had used it this morning to carry the supermarket bundles, and now she cursed her own bullheadedness for having retired it immediately to its berth. Laden with bulky parcels, she was cold and cross. Damn her own stubbornness! And damn him, she swore under billowing white breath!

Her date with Tom McCann that evening was pleasant. Tom was a live wire, and provided fun and laughter. After a simple dinner at her apartment, he took her to a production by the five-college theater group of Chekhov's *Uncle Vanya,* then to a coffeehouse in nearby Amherst. It was only at the end of the evening, during the inevitable goodnight kiss, that her mind began to wander. As she leaned back against her bolted front door, having sent the mathematics professor on his way with as enthusiastic a thank you as she could muster under the circumstances, she thought of Max's kiss, its hunger, its challenge, its reward. By comparison Tom's paled sadly. Instinctively, she knew that future suitors would meet the same fate. Maxwell Kraig was a man above others, in so many ways.

Sleep was elusive that night, as peace of mind had been elusive that day. When finally it overtook her in the early morning hours, it was fitful and disturbed. Only after she woke at seven to the unceremonious thump of the Sunday paper at her front door, did she finally fall into a sound slumber. She was not ready for the doorbell when its harsh squeal speared her oblivion at nine thirty. Ignoring it did no good; the heavy hand that activated it was persistent, bearing down

59

every thirty seconds such that she was wide awake and very grumpy by the fifth ring. Angrily, she slammed out of bed, thudded barefoot through the living room to the front hall, where she stood at the top of the stairs and yelled irritably, "Who is it?"

"Florist," came the distant reply, and she swore in exasperation as she plodded down the narrow staircase, furious at whoever had the gall to send flowers at such an early hour. She unbolted the door and indignantly bent to scoop up the newspaper and toss it onto the stair behind her before irascibly facing the delivery.

It was indeed a florist's box that was held out to her, but this was no golden-winged FTD Mercury. Rather, it was a devilishly handsome, sheepskin-coated Max Kraig, eyeing her so strangely that she wondered whether she had suddenly grown horns. Then in a fit of mortification, she realized that she had come straight from bed. Her hair was loose and disheveled, her face scrubbed bare of all makeup, her eyes still groggy from the sleep which had shrouded her not five minutes before. To make matters worse, she was clothed only in an ankle-length flannel nightshirt, high-collared and long-sleeved, with soft Victorian ruffles at neck, wrist, and foot. She was primly covered, to be sure, yet it was her nightgown!

With a gasp of horror, she slammed the door shut on that most good-looking face, closing her eyes tightly as she willed the freshly groomed visage to disappear into the crisp morning air. Slumping back against the door, she opened her eyes and glanced frantically about her. What was he doing here? What right did he have to shatter the peace of her Sunday morning? It was bad enough that he had intruded on her thoughts yesterday, but this was unfair! Why was he here? And what right did he have to see her like this? As she struggled with the predicament, the doorbell rang again and again.

"Laura, open the door!" he called loudly, as she impulsively muffled the sound with a hand at either ear.

"Go away! It's too early!" she answered his call with a loud and panicked one of her own.

"It's after nine thirty. I've purposely waited this late. It won't take long. Now open the door!" A renewed assault on the doorbell punctuated his words. "Laura, it's cold out—" His voice broke off in midsentence as Laura simultaneously heard the heavy sound of the door next to hers. Mrs. Daniels!

Without further thought she yanked at her own door, shoved open the storm door, and all but dragged Max in by a bulky sleeve, too disturbed to note the dazzling smile he sent toward the face at the adjoining doorway as he was drawn past it, out of the cold, into the small hallway.

Ill humor mixed with embarrassment to produce raw fury. Hands on hips, Laura confronted Max. "Just what do you think you're doing here?" Without a word, he held out the florist box. "What is this supposed to be?" she demanded testily as she glanced at the long, thin box before lifting her eyes once more to his face. And what a long way up it was, she suddenly realized, standing barefoot as she was before this imposing giant.

"A peace offering." His voice was maddeningly velvet.

61

"For what?" The fury had already begun to melt against her will.

Deep chocolate eyes swept her face as he explained. "I . . . was rather rude when I slammed out of the library the other night. I owe you an apology."

"You don't fool me for a minute," she retorted, clutching at the remnants of anger to cover her growing self-consciousness. "You just wanted to catch me off guard." Had that been his intention, he had been totally successful. She felt perfectly foolish and utterly vulnerable standing there so helplessly beneath his penetrating gaze. She lifted a nervous hand to push back a wayward strand of shiny black hair.

"Actually," he baited her boldly, "I was curious to see whether you spent the night alone."

The fury returned. "Oh, you were, were you? Well," she began, sarcasm heavy on her glib tongue, "it so happens that my man is still in bed. Ramon!" She shrieked defiantly back over her shoulder. "Ramon!"

Max grinned, that irresistibly devastating grin of his, as he scored her head to toe. "You know, I might have believed you if you'd pulled that one before you opened the door. But now . . ." He put the box down and opened the buttons of his heavy jacket. Although he was merely making himself comfortable, his action distracted Laura.

She was instantly fascinated by the teal color of his V-neck cashmere sweater, the fine fit of his darker corduroy slacks. Her obvious examination and approval was not missed by its object, a satisfied light entering his eyes as he went on.

"But now that I see you wearing that, I'd never be able to believe your charade."

An unwelcome flush crept to Laura's pale cheeks. "What's wrong with . . . this?" Indignantly, she held out the loose folds of her gown. To add to her embarrassment, Max threw his head back in a hearty laugh.

"Oh, nothing's wrong with it." He composed himself enough to elaborate. "It's just a little too . . . prim . . . for a tigress!"

"I'm no tigress," she snorted quickly as she looked away in renewed humiliation.

"Oh, no?" His deeply seductive tone brought her eyes back to his, which made another foray over her largely hidden figure before climbing again. "I've seen you very proper at the office, very elegant at that fundraiser, and now very innocent here. But I know there's a tigress deep within that very proper exterior. If there had been a Ramon upstairs, you would not be wearing this . . . frock!" He took a step closer and put a hand out to finger the lace at her neckline, his eyes caressing her softness in a way that held her speechless. It was the same hypnotic state which had begun to weaken her, first erasing any anger and stilling all resistance, then holding her entranced as his nearness kindled those delicious fiery feelings within her.

"You know," he teased in a near-whisper, "about the only thing that stays the same is your nail polish." He took one of her hands in his and lifted her fingertips to his lips, lightly kissing them, then placing her hand palm down against his newly shaven cheek. "And this . . ." His lips lowered to hers and those fiery feelings burst into flame, sending a tremor of desire through her.

Of its own volition her hand moved from his

cheek to his jawline, tracing it lightly as her mouth clung to his for the moment.

"Sensuous Burgundy," she murmured breathlessly against the thumb which had begun to outline her lips.

His tantalizing caress stilled for a puzzled instant. "What?"

A grin surfaced out of her passion-coated daze. "Sensuous Burgundy . . . my nails," she repeated impishly, then laughed at the triviality of the information.

For a long moment he stood and looked down at her, the light of desire illuminating his mellow brown eyes. "That's fitting," he concluded huskily. "Sensuous Burgundy . . . and the tigress. Both go with you everywhere, one without, one within."

As his voice faded to a hushed stillness, the smiles also faded. It seemed a moment of truth. For Laura the decision had been made during those sleepless hours when she accepted the profound effect this man had on her. She had to pursue the relationship; some unknown force bid her do so. For Max the decision had been reached in a similar manner, culminating in his arrival at the flower shop to purchase the single pink long-stemmed rose which now lay, forgotten for the moment, in its box at the foot of the stairs.

"Come here." A hoarse whisper broke the silence, a redundant command as Max put a large hand to Laura's waist and drew her flannel-clad form against him, within the warm comfort of his sheepskin jacket, within the protective circle of his arms. She wound her own arms inside the jacket and around his back as she buried her face against his throat, his clean and manly scent drugging her. A quiver surged through her veins as his hands explored the soft lines of her back, her waist, her hips.

"My God," he exclaimed in a half-whisper, "you've got nothing on underneath this, do you?" It was an accusation to which she could only plead guilty. Drawing her head back to look up at him, she shrugged.

Where her senses had gone, she had no idea. She knew that she should go up and dress, yet she had no desire to. At least she should back out of Max's devastating embrace, but she had no desire to do that either. Failing all else, she should have spoken up in protest of what seemed forthcoming, yet words eluded her. In the next instant breath eluded her too, as she was lifted into the cradle of Max's arms and carried up the stairs to be placed on her own two feet only when he had reached the soft living room carpet.

The eyes that melted into hers were tender, countering the faint tautness in his voice. "You'd better go get a robe and some slippers, or you'll catch cold." They were not the words she had expected, not by a long shot. And accompanied as they were by a kiss on the forehead, she felt strangely rejected. Whether he saw the hurt look in her eyes, she did not know, for he turned to retrieve the newspaper and the flower, and she turned and slowly headed for her bedroom.

As she opened the closet door and stepped into her furry mules, Laura wondered what *she* had wanted to happen. Puzzled, she wasn't quite sure. Slowly, she padded to the side of her bed and sank onto the rumpled pink sheets, staring blindly at the frost patterns on the windowpane. Funny, she hadn't thought that far in advance. She had only known divine ecstasy when he touched her, held her, kissed her. The pulsing knot that demanded more was an enigma.

The form that entered her periphery startled her. Looking up in surprise, she saw Max approaching, walking softly to where she sat, his eyes studying her subtly. As she gazed up at him, the familiar force seized her. Yet something held her back—was it fear of further rejection . . . or fear of the opposite?

The bed yielded to Max's weight as he sat down, facing her. A large hand took her face and held it gently as he kissed her, slowly and thoroughly, his tongue delivering shivers of desire as it traced the soft fullness of her lips, then explored her mouth's recesses.

Her breathing was heavy, as was his, when he released her. Impulsively, and in a gesture of innocence, she pulled her legs beneath her until she was kneeling opposite him. With her face now higher, she studied his, feature by feature, in unhurried wonder, her hands finding the thickness of his hair and burying themselves in it.

She made no protest as he sought the buttons of her nightshirt, releasing them one by one until there was a narrow flesh-toned slit from neck to waist. His eyes flickered to hers for a sign of objection, and when there was none, he reached up, took both of her hands from his neck and gently lowered them. Then in a motion slowed by adoration, he slid the flannel off her shoulders, pushing it down until her arms were freed.

If Laura felt any shyness at sitting half-naked before him, it was put to rest by the heartrending tenderness of his gaze. "How can one woman be so beautiful!" he murmured, stretching a hand out to outline the circle of her breast. She bit her lip to stifle the outcry of delight that surged at his intimacy. Lifting her hands once more to his shoulders, she drew herself closer, desperately needing a more binding touch than this first, painfully teasing one.

Sensing her need, Max took her into his arms, crushing her breasts against the softness of his sweater, as he reclaimed her lips, kissing her now with a hunger that belied his outward calm. Gently, he eased her down onto the bed before he released her lips to rain kisses on her neck and throat, then on her breasts. This time she gasped aloud when his lips touched her nipple, tantalizing a rosy bud with his tongue as his hand gently possessed its taut mate.

Laura had never dreamed of the height to which he took her with his caresses, driving her out of her mind with pleasure as he made his own every inch of the flesh exposed to him. She thought of nothing but how much she trusted this man, how much she wanted him, how very good he made her feel when he touched her.

The abrupt jangle of the telephone filtered through the haze of passion once, then twice, and a third time before Max's voice joined it. "You'd better get that." There was something in his tone that brought Laura tumbling off her high-flying cloud.

"It's not important," she suggested wishfully.

Max levered himself to look soberly down at her. "I think you'd better answer it."

Fearful and suspicious at once, she groaned, "You didn't leave *my* number with your service, did you?"

He didn't budge. "I don't have a service. Are you going to answer it, Laura, or shall I?"

It was all he needed to say. She was not yet ready to explain his presence in her home to herself, let alone someone else. Sliding quickly out from beneath his arms, she crammed her own back into the sleeves of her nightshirt, buttoning it as she made for the kitchen where the phone rang relentlessly.

"Hello," she barked into the receiver, then steadied her voice immediately when she heard the identification. "Yes, Sergeant Adams . . . when was he taken into custody? . . . The charge? . . . Past record? . . . Where is he from? . . . Do you have verification? Let's say $50,000 . . . no, I don't want him running around on the streets. Fine . . . yes, thank you, Sergeant."

By the time she hung up, Max had returned to the living room and had begun to thumb through the newspaper. "Any problem?" he called, catching her eye.

She shook her head, intending her answer only for the phone call. "Some fellow has been arrested. Assault and battery with a dangerous weapon. They needed someone to set bail until the arraignment tomorrow morning."

"Do you get calls like that often?"

"Every now and then," she answered. Then she heard the sadness in her own voice as she added, "But not usually at as inopportune a time." Realistically, she knew that the moment was gone. Perhaps it was a blessing. If so, why did she feel such profound disappointment? "Would you like some coffee?" she asked, the only practical thing she could think of to say.

Max still studied her, his eyes dark and unfathomable. "Only if you'll have some."

Without another word she set up the coffee maker, then stood back to watch it drip. The only sound from the other room was the occasional rustle of the newspaper. When the thin dark stream of steaming liquid had ceased to fall, she filled two mugs, then walked back into the living room, handing one to Max over the back of the sofa.

An eyebrow arched as he took the mug. "How do you know I take it black?"

She shrugged her shoulders nonchalantly, as she sat against the top of the sofa. "You had it that way at the party. I never forget a fellow purist!" Could she tell him that she remembered every such detail where he was concerned?

The paper was suddenly gone from his lap. "Laura," he began, a faint frown thinning his lips, "you're a virgin, aren't you?"

She hadn't been prepared for this line of questioning. "What does *that* have to do with anything?" she snapped sharply, her blue eyes widening in accusation.

Max's gaze did not falter. "It has everything to do with what's happening." Then in answer to the muted skepticism on her face, he went on softly. "I would have gladly taken you a minute ago. You know that, don't you?" If he had expected a simple yes or no, he had underestimated the will of the woman before him.

Cagey she was not; she could not hide the deep hurt that bewildered her. "Why didn't you?"

There was a subtle hardening of his features; for a moment, Laura thought she had angered him. Then in a sudden movement he stood up and walked to the fireplace, keeping his back to her as he put one arm on the mantelpiece. The stretch of his sweater over the solid muscles of his back quickened Laura's pulse.

"I don't know." It was small consolation to hear this paragon of competence make such a statement. She had assumed that Max always knew what he wanted and why he hadn't taken advantage of her when she was at her most defenseless, even willing, was a puzzlement.

His voice was low and smooth, its tension gone when he turned to face her. "I don't know," he repeated, an element of near defeat in his walk as he rounded the back of the sofa and stopped to look down at her. His eyes held the same warmth she had come to know, yet a distant quality had replaced the smoldering passion to which she had thrilled earlier.

His fingers held his mug as defensively as she held hers, using it as a makeshift substitute for the touching this closeness tempted. A thread of regret hung in the air, a sense of loss which Laura, for one, felt acutely.

"I have to leave now, Laura," he finally spoke, drawing himself up a little straighter in an effort to break the intangible bond that held him before her. Pride kept her from asking why, despite the voice within her that screamed it, and she somehow managed a smile. As she stood to walk with him to the stairs she felt the warm band of his arm slip behind her shoulders to draw her close once more.

"I'll talk with you later in the week to set up a pretrial conference. I'd like to have this trial scheduled and over as soon as possible. Be good," he murmured, his lips brushing the top of her head for a moment before he released her, and throwing his coat across his shoulders, he started down the stairs.

He had gone but halfway when he stopped, turned to her, the devilment which so affected her once more in his eyes, and grinned playfully. "Don't forget to put that flower in water, tigress!" Before she could catch her breath the door had shut, leaving her with the memory of how he had looked at that last moment—tall and well-built, dark and daring, infinitely handsome, and totally endearing in the most masculine of ways.

It was a picture she carried with her for the rest of the day, particularly vivid when she looked at the solitary rose, long-stemmed and newly opening, which had been his peace offering. The situation was ironic, she mused. While his gesture had been suitably apologetic for his harsh words at the library, it had led to new developments that shattered any peace of mind Laura might have wished for. The clouded abyss loomed deeper, the mist growing denser with each lost foothold, the rock bottom an awesome mystery which held either ecstasy or misery, but hint of neither along the way.

For Laura, who prided herself in her high level of self-control and self-understanding, it was an agonizing maelstrom in which she floundered. Her primary principle of separating office from home had been broken, due to an internal weakness she had not even known she possessed. When she was with Max she forgot all but his devastating appeal. But, she realized with a start, the appeal had ceased to be the purely physical one that had so captured her on that first day. The biological attraction was still there, but it

71

had now been joined by so many other things that the pull was stronger each time she saw him.

And the attraction was not onesided. Max seemed as taken with her, at times, as she was with him. He drew her out, enjoyed talking with her, listening to her talk. And his own words confirmed that he found her physically attractive. Why then had he held back? Why had he insisted she answer that telephone, knowing her own heightened state of arousal, as well as his?

That disruptive call had been a strategically timed reminder that for the time being at least, work would have to supersede any other relationship she might wish to have with Max. There were upcoming meetings, then the trial, all of which would demand her utmost concentration. There was no room for romance in the courtroom.

Four

On one thing Laura and Max were in complete agreement: The trial should be scheduled as soon as possible. For only when it was over would she be able to realistically assess her feelings for this compelling man. Only when it was over would she be able to resolve the nagging inner tug-of-war between lawyer and woman. In the meanwhile she vowed to keep private meetings between Max and herself at a minimum. If there were others present, it might be possible to avoid a reminder of the awesome physical attraction that ignited into fiery passion at the slightest provocation.

In this matter Laura was only partially successful. Over the next few weeks there were numerous meetings between the prosecution and the defense of the Stallway case. On each of those occasions Laura carefully planned to have other parties present. Often Sandy Chatfield played the unobtrusive role of her bodyguard, a most natural choice considering his involvement in the case. During the pretrial conference itself, it was the D.A. who sat in as Laura and Max turned over witness statements, physical and scientific reports, and Laura supplied Max with the transcript of the grand jury hearings.

Indeed there was always a third or fourth party with them, yet this added presence, while inhibiting any actual physical contact between prosecutor and defender, did in no way lessen the intensity of the visual interchange between the two. Laura's hopes of remaining neutral to Max's charm were dashed on the smoldering pyre of his gaze. Be it across the room, over the desk, or through an open door, the effect remained the same. She was ever aware of him, of his warm chocolate gaze branding her a woman even as his more impartial words dealt with her as a lawyer.

To her chagrin it was far from a one-way visual seduction. Laura's own eyes were a blue flame, dancing at the sight of a strong, note-taking hand, its manly wisps of dark hair curling out from beneath the cuff of his shirt, at the suggestion of the sinuous bulge of a shoulder beneath the same, at the fall of dark hair across the finely creased forehead. In light of these powerful distractions, it was an even greater challenge to maintain the outwardly impervious attitude of the professional. Thankfully, Laura rose to the occasion, as did Max.

If she'd ever had doubts as to his legal comportment, they were dispelled from the first, when he proved to be a courteous and able negotiator. Laura had never dealt with one as concise and clear-thinking. He knew what he needed to shape his case and how to go about getting it. Contrary to so many other experiences she'd had, Max seemed unbothered that, as a lawyer, she was of the opposite sex; there was none of the macho-motivated arrogance she had come to despise. Opposite Max, she thoroughly enjoyed being a lawyer. When she held her own on certain issues, he respected her reasoning, not wasting time arguing pointlessly, and on principle alone, for what was secondary.

It was a lesson that spoke strongly to Laura's own personal dilemma, the urgency of which was not eased by these sessions. And, when each was over and Max had returned to Boston, there was always that inexplicable feeling of emptiness.

Through these conferences, and more specifically, through the more casual lunches or coffee breaks that accompanied them, Laura gained insight not only into the man as a lawyer, but into the man as a person. In one such instance the D.A. had sat in during the morning's session, then the three had walked to the soup-and-sandwich restaurant near the courthouse.

"I understand the Civil Liberties Union has approached you on that school matter." Frank addressed Max after they had ordered lunch.

Max laughed quietly, a deep and throaty chuckle which Laura found to be absolutely musical. "Word spreads like wildfire in this state, doesn't it!" He cast a sidelong glance at Laura, whose questioning gaze told of her own ignorance on the subject. He started to explain when the D.A. cut him short, taking that job on himself.

"The counselor has been asked to represent a group of children and their parents who are bringing charges of abuse and neglect against the Wilkins Home for Retarded Children. It is still in the talking stage from what I hear. Is that correct, Max?" he asked, turning his attention back to the dark man on his left.

That dark man looked even darker as he suddenly took on a brooding mien. "You've got it," he confirmed tersely.

Curiosity impelled Laura to join the discussion. "I must be out of it, but I don't recall hearing about this. What are the specific charges?" Her question was directed to Max from a totally personal viewpoint. Her knowledge of the Wilkins Home was limited to occasional newspaper reports and one heartrending visit she had made several years before to the facility as a college student participating in a forum on the mentally retarded. Memory conjured up images of gray buildings, as drab and illkept within as without, worn and inadequate furnishings, an undertrained and shorthanded staff—in short, a pathetic situation. A year after her visit, entirely unrelated to it, there had been a complete overhaul of the home, with long-time personnel being replaced by a newer, supposedly more sympathetic and progressive group.

Sensing her human interest, Max explained patiently, if somberly. "There have been claims of corporal punishment and gross mistreatment

75

of the more severely ill children, not to mention those more self-sufficient who are left to their own devices for hour after hour."

"But I thought with the new administrators and trained personnel—" she began, puzzled.

Max interrupted vehemently, the slashes by the corners of his mouth turning down in disgust at his own opinion of the Wilkins Home. "All of whom are so wrapped up in their sophisticated theories of treatment that they have no *idea* how to deal with the reality of the retarded children in their care." His voice lowered, as did his gaze. "My heart goes out to those kids!"

It was an awakening experience for Laura, this evidence of such deep feeling in Max. Even more surprising was his reaction to the D.A.'s follow-up.

"Will you take the case?" Frank buttonholed him, eying him with the shrewd, political air which was part and parcel of the D.A.'s job. "It is an explosive case to bring to trial. Great publicity. A real gem to add to your treasury . . . not that your career needs any help." He chuckled.

Max did not share his humor. "I don't give a damn about my career! This is an explosive case because the bastards who are responsible for those helpless children and to their nearly-as-helpless parents should be behind bars!"

Laura stared mutely at him, amazed by his forcefulness and equally as impressed. This was, indeed, the type of case that the illustrious Maxwell Kraig would be expected to try. Yet, whereas once Laura might have suspected his motives to be similar to those the D.A. had mentioned, now she saw deep commitment as the motivating force.

"I'm sorry, Laura." Max's velvety voice sifted through the sounds in the restaurant. "You'll have to excuse my language, but I find my patience hard to control on this issue." His jaw had tensed visibly into a square; Laura wondered whether much of his anger wasn't directed at Frank for his callous inference. In this she agreed with Max. For the first time, she began to understand the bitterness the good-looking lawyer had expressed the day they had met, when he referred to the public image that was his life.

There was a gentle softness in her voice now, a shaft of support in her blue eyes as she sought to ease his anger. "You've got to try that case," she informed him. "Only someone who feels so strongly about the plight of those children could give them the representation they need." Her words were heartfelt, and as such, brought an immediate softening to Max's features. His smile said the only thank you that was needed; his eyes said the rest, burning into her soul. For that brief moment, they communicated without words or touch. It was as though they had forgotten the presence of the third, until he conspicuously cleared his throat, then changed the subject as the waitress brought their food. Laura participated only marginally in the rest of the conversation, so intent was she on assimilating this new side of Maxwell Kraig.

By the second week in February the major matters relating to the Stallway case had been settled. Laura was pleased with the official outcome of her meetings with Max, although she would have liked to have more time to prepare for the trial itself, given her own heavy caseload, than the late March date would allow. But Max's arguments were valid; the boy had a right to a speedy trial. And Laura knew that she would welcome the conclusion of this particular trial. It was inevitable that she should feel some trepidation in trying her first murder case; the fact that Max was the defense attorney both enhanced the excitement and aggravated the anticipation.

For there had been one side-effect of their meetings on which Laura had not counted—the agonizing physical frustration that assailed her after each one—at night, on the weekends, in her imagination, both day and night. He made no further overtures into her personal realm, though there wasn't a weekend morning that she did not hold her breath upon awakening, half-hoping that he would be on her doorstep. All too vivid in her memory were the protectiveness of his arms, the gentleness of his hands, the persuasion of his lips, the strength of his manliness. If he missed her, in this most intimate sense, she would never know. Ruefully, she concluded that she had refused his dinner invitation once too often, for he had not risked refusal again. And, yes, she had wanted him to. It was a sad irony, she mused one cold and rainy Sunday afternoon as she half-heartedly appliqued Valentines onto each of the T-shirts she'd bought for her kids, to be presented during class the following Saturday. She wanted to be with Max, to share with him in ways she'd never imagined. Yet there was that basic conflict between wanting him and wanting to avoid involvement with him. The only clear thing was the increasing sense of unfulfillment that shadowed her.

In a desperate effort to sort her thoughts, she put in a call to her brother, to whom she had always, as a child, poured out her heart. In a fortunate twist of fate, he'd had tentative plans to visit a new friend and fellow linguist, a young woman, in Albany. It would take simply a short detour to Northampton for him to visit his "favorite sister." Laura was ecstatic. The date was set for Friday, the plans calling for Jack to stay over with her before continuing on to Albany on Saturday.

True to his word, Jack arrived at Laura's apartment in time for a special dinner she had prepared—his favorite recipe of chicken cacciatore over rice with a huge salad. And, true to his word, he opened his ears while Laura told him everything there was to know about Maxwell Kraig, from the most significant arraignment to the most recent conferences. It was a picture of compelling interest and overwhelming desire she painted of her reaction to him, sparing her brother only the intimate details of the passionate encounters that burned so brightly in her memory.

Despite their father's acquaintance with Max, Jack had never met him, knowing only vaguely of him. He listened intently, questioning her intermittently until she ran out of words and lapsed into an exhausted silence. It was an air of self-pity that had overtaken her, sparked by the seeming contradiction of her feelings. She was jolted by her brother's gut response.

"It sounds like you're falling in love." The

concern in his voice did nothing to dull the impaling action of his words.

"What? Of course not!" She denied it with unnecessary force before self-doubt seized her. "At least I don't think so," she added more calmly, absently fingering the folds of the linen napkin on her lap. Her long lashes flickered as she raised her eyes once more to her brother's gentle face. "How could I be, Jack? I don't know him all that well. I've never gone out with him. I don't even know what kind of car he drives, who his friends are, how his apartment is decorated . . ."

Jack's skepticism was heavy. "You're evading the issue, little sister. Those things don't make a bit of difference, and you know it! The only thing that really counts, *really counts,* is you and he together. Does it work?"

Long moments of silence passed before Laura answered. "I don't know," she began softly. "I think it does . . . for me, at any rate." Her mind was filled with images of spending her life with Max, and even given her limited knowledge of him, she found the prospect, among other things, exciting. But there was so much she didn't know. Suddenly she looked up, angry at her own unsureness. "This has never happened to me, Jack! I have no idea how to handle it. I still have that case to try against him . . ." Her voice trailed off as she shook her head in frustration.

Recognizing her confusion, her brother kept his tone patient and understanding. "Do you really want my opinion, Laura?" She looked up at him in anticipation, her expression answer enough to his query. "I think you have to give him a chance. Go out with him. You were really stubborn about refusing his invitations . . . and foolish. Sometimes, hon, you have to put things into perspective. And from the sounds of it, the man is something extra special to you, which even your precious career has no right to deny. No, hear me out." He spoke in expectance of the protest that was already forming on Laura's pouting lips. "You've been a . . . prig. I'm sorry, but that's the best word to describe it. Laura, there's more to life than law. And you really don't have to make the choice between love and a career; millions of women have both nowadays. Let go! Relax! Be the woman that you want to be!"

Laura could be silenced no longer. "But, Jack, I have to try this case opposite him! How can I be the levelheaded prosecutor when every time I look at him I melt, my knees get weak, I begin to quake inside?" She bolted out of her seat and walked to the far end of the table, looking back at her brother with an air of defeat. "I'm supposed to be picturing the evidence, and all I can picture is his face just before he kisses me. How do I cope with that, Jack?" She eyed him beseechingly, then followed his movement to where she stood.

Putting his hands on her shoulders in a gesture of brotherly comfort, he calmed her quietly. "You relax, for one thing. Getting yourself all worked up is not going to help. Just let things happen, Laura. If he asks you out, go out with him. You never can tell," he added with a glint of humor, "he may turn out to be a total bore after the first date."

Laura turned a cynical eye on him. "You've never met Max," she retorted. "And anyway, I doubt he'll ask me out again. I think he's decided

he doesn't want to go out with a . . . prig."
Guiltily, she owned up to her brother's assertion,
then was actually able to laugh with him when
he enveloped her in an affectionate bear hug.

"You never can tell about men," he murmured
by way of backhanded encouragement. "They're
a strange breed."

Laura was to discover just that the following
morning. Jack slept in the second bedroom. After
a breakfast of eggs Benedict, a favorite of Laura's
but one which she would not dream of preparing
just for herself and therefore rarely had, Jack
repacked his suitcase and headed for his car.
Throwing her heavy fur jacket over the wool
turtleneck and jeans she had unceremoniously
donned for breakfast, she walked with him
outside, standing by in the cold February air as
he stowed the bag in his trunk, then gave her a
final hug of affection before he started out.

Laura waved until his car rounded the corner
and disappeared from sight. Only then did she
see the Mercedes parked across the street, and
its owner, his brown hair and sheepskin jacket
instantly identifiable, as he slowly emerged from
the driver's seat.

Rendered speechless by a blend of excitement,
relief, and anxiety, she stood motionless on the
sidewalk as he approached. The angry glint in
his eyes was the first thing that throttled her, his
contemptuous expression the next, as he drew
himself to his full height directly before her.

"It's an experience to sit outside your place for
five minutes. I didn't bargain on seeing last
night's stud leaving, suitcase in hand, no less!"
he burst out in scathing proclamation. Laura felt
a chill spear her, as an icy blast filtered through

to her ever nerve end. Before she could find the words of denial, Max's voice took on a taunting tone. "Innocent Laura! I should have guessed it was all an act. Too much of a tigress to be caged for so long. And to think," he barrelled on stormily, "that I sat outside for those five minutes trying to find the courage to approach you again. You're shrewd, all right. You held me off with that damned look of purity. What a fool I am!"

It was the utter contempt in his eyes that set Laura's stomach churning. She turned and dashed toward the house, stopping at the doorstep only when the firm hand on her arm halted her escape.

"Where do you think you're running to? I haven't finished—"

She could no longer bear the fury in his gaze, so disturbed was she by his diatribe. With a trembling hand she waved off his restraining arm. "I don't feel well . . . I'm going in . . . please, let me go." Struck by both the pleading whisper of her voice and the pallor of her skin, he released her. Sensing freedom, she ran through the door and up the stairs, not quite sure that her trembling knees would carry her all the way, until she collapsed into the sofa and hung her head low, her major concern being to muster the strength to get to the bathroom. To her relief the wave of nausea passed, leaving her only with a thunderously pounding heartbeat and an overall weakness.

"Are you all right?" There was no trace of anger in the voice that came to her, no fury in the hand that gently massaged her neck.

Was she all right? What had happened to her? Why had Max's attack on her affected her so violently? After hoping, day after day, that he would appear at her apartment just as he had, how could she allow him such a misconception?

Without further deliberation she looked up at his face, blurred now through the tears that misted her vision yet refused to fall. "It was my brother, Jack. He came in last night. I . . . needed him. He stayed in the spare room and is on his way to see his girlfriend in Albany." She hadn't taken a breath during her speech, had merely let the words flow as quickly as possible. Now she buried her face in her hands as she sought to control her spasmodic breathing.

In the next conscious movement she was pulled, fur jacket and all, into Max's arms, sheepskin jacket and all. Her head rested against his sweatered chest, her arms were pinned between their bodies as he gently rocked her back and forth.

"I'm sorry, baby. So sorry." His deep-timbred choice of endearment made her melt even deeper into him, her upset vanishing as his arms maintained their healing touch. "It was stupid of me to go on like that," he reproached himself, as his tone grew lower and more husky. "I've waited so long to see you alone. . . . I've wanted to call you so many times. When I saw him leaving with his bag, hugging you, I've never been as furious"—he drew back to look down at her— "or as jealous!"

At that instant Laura knew that her brother was not too far from the truth. She was falling in love with Max! It felt so good to be with him like this! When he bent his head to kiss her, she felt the shudder pass from his body to hers. What was he feeling, she wondered, as she gave herself freely to the passion of his kiss. For a mere instant she pretended that his vibrations were alive with love, guiding her into delirious happiness. If only . . .

"Forgive me?" He asked, his voice a gentle murmur against her lips.

Once again she was lost in his magnetism. Her own voice surprised her when it whispered in hoarse response, "Only if you kiss me once more." And he did, warmly and eagerly, making up for those long moments of frustration that had characterized the last few weeks. When finally he set her away from him, he appeared to be struggling with some inner torment.

"What is it?" she whispered.

"You! What am I going to do with you? You haunt me night and day when I'm away from you, then you tease me mercilessly when I'm here. You are a tease, you know, pulling stunts like that one-more-kiss bit!" Laura blushed under his penetrating gaze, her heart pealing with happiness at the tone of affection that came through his feigned annoyance. "There you go again with that maidenly blush!" he growled in adamant support of his claim. But before she could begin to control the color in her cheeks, he floored her again in a voice thick with desire.

"Let me make love to you, Laura." His eyes bore a burning hunger with their sober plea. The masculine aura about him set fire to Laura's senses, exciting her even as it frightened her. "I'd take you to bed right now, if you'd let me." His voice was deep and smooth, crooning his desire, his long fingers splayed through the hair on either side of her face.

He felt the hesitation in her body before she

said a word. But the compulsion to explain was too strong. "Max, part of me wants that more than anything else at this moment," she began, "but, then, part of me is . . . afraid."

Misinterpreting her words, he grew infinitely tender and supportive. "There's nothing to be frightened of, Laura. It would be so very, very beautiful—"

"That's not what I mean," she cut in quickly, flustered by his misunderstanding. "I'm frightened of my own feelings, and what would happen afterward. There are so many things to be considered." She shook her head in confusion, recalling vividly the discussion she'd had with her brother. "It's all happening so quickly. I just need . . . a little more time."

Displaying once more an uncanny awareness of her thoughts, Max let his hands fall from her face and stood up from the sofa, removing his jacket and tossing it onto a nearby chair. "You said that your brother was here because you needed him. What did you mean?" His gaze examined her every feature as she stood to walk to the window.

Shielded from his prodding gaze, she hesitated for long moments before gathering her courage to answer him honestly. "I was confused—about you, about me, about the trial. Jack and I have always been able to talk. So we did."

"And?" The voice was directly behind her, velvet-edged and strong.

Wrapping both arms about her middle, she elaborated. "He helped me to see some things, others are still foggy." She turned with sudden boldness to face him. "Jack says that I've been wrong about refusing to go out with you . . ."

A glint of humor flicked in Max's eye. "I like your brother already. He must have inherited the common sense," he quipped in lighthearted reference to the not-so-lighthearted accusation he'd made in the courthouse library.

A smile found its way through the mask of unsureness, as Laura made her shy confession. "I think he may be right."

There was neither arrogance nor smugness in the response. "I know he is, but you may have a point too, as much as I hate to admit it. If things are happening too quickly," Max explained, his hands now rubbing Laura's upper arms, "then we'll just slow them down. It's going to be difficult for me," he added, the devilish gleam in his eye dissolving to an excited sparkle, "but I want you too badly to risk any discomfort for you."

His sincerity touched her, knotting her throat to preclude response. Mercifully, Max took over in his commanding fashion.

"But, if I'm prepared to wait, you've got to meet me halfway," he growled amiably. Laura's arched eyebrow spurred him on. "Three things. First you'll spend today with me."

"But I have to shop, to teach—" She protested feebly.

"Then *I'll* spend today with *you.*" Head and voice lowered simultaneously. "You're not getting away from me so easily. Then, second," he continued with growing enjoyment at the shaping plans, "we're going out to dinner tonight. Alone. Just you and me. Understood?"

Delighted submission was the rule as Laura quietly nodded her head. "And the third thing?" Having already precluded a night of lovemaking, the third was a mystery. She stood expectantly as he reached into a back pocket and pulled out a small, flat box.

"Third, you will accept my contribution to Valentine's Day." There was smug satisfaction written over his features as she stared at him. Then slowly she took the box, carefully removed its gay red-and-white wrapping, raised the lid and removed a small pendant on an exquisite gold chain, a delicate gold heart embedded with a sparkling ruby.

"It's magnificent!" Tears of pleasure found their way, unbidden, to eyes of China blue.

The irresistible grin shone anew. "I thought the ruby would go well with your nail polish. That's perfect . . . Sensuous Burgundy." He threw back his head in laughter at the reminder of the earlier conversation. When the laughter ended, Laura spoke, her voice emotion-filled.

"Thank you, Max. It's beautiful. I'll always treasure it!" She unconsciously clutched the necklace in the hand held over her heart. At his pantomimed suggestion, she lifted the weight of her hair and allowed him to fasten the clasp, leaving the heart to fall gracefully to the hollow of her throat. At that instant she felt the heady sensation of lips against her neck. She would have burst with delight had it not been for Max's change of tempo.

He clapped his hands for attention and put forth his inquiry. "Now then, what is on the agenda for today? I think we've wasted enough time on the preliminaries." The double meaning of his word was not lost on Laura, who sent him a dazzling smile before reeling off the things to be done.

While he read the morning paper, she cleaned

up the kitchen, quickly made her bed, stripped the cot her brother had used, and ran down to the basement to put in a load of laundry. As she went from chore to chore, the small gold heart served as a reminder of the tall, dark man awaiting her patiently.

"All set!" she finally declared, returning to the living room to retrieve her jacket and her date (what a satisfying title), stopping but briefly at her landlady's door for a shopping list and money before allowing Max to drive her to the supermarket. Suitably impressed by the simple though luxurious interior of the Mercedes, she peered through the shade of long lashes at the profile of her chauffeur.

"It seems almost sacrilegious to take this car to the market." She smirked.

Max kept his eyes on the road, following the direction of her pointing finger. "It's not the first time. I have to eat too."

Curiosity aroused, she cornered him. "I would have thought you'd have someone—cook, houseboy, maid—to do that type of thing."

His mouth twisted into a grimace. "That's the image, isn't it?"

Recognizing her error and his prior bitterness on the topic, Laura steered a more positive course. "Are you a good cook?"

He shrugged, smiling gently. "Fair to middlin'. Maybe you'll get a chance to sample my culinary talents one day." He reached out to take her hand in an easy squeeze.

"I'd like that," she answered softly as they pulled into the parking lot.

How the mundane ritual of food shopping could have taken on such a romantic air was an amazement to Laura, who was ever aware of the tall figure beside her, as well as of the familiar faces that greeted her, then sent admiring glances toward her handsome companion.

When the food had been returned to the house—Mrs. Daniels' to her, and accepted with a once-over to the man who delivered it—unpacked, and stowed, they headed toward the center of Northampton and the sports shop that had been holding a new tennis racquet for Laura. Encouraged by the sense of frivolity that danced within her, she then fell in love with a newly arrived tennis dress, which she promptly tried on and impulsively modeled for her most appreciative audience.

"Not bad, for a lawyer," was the official statement, the approval in the chocolate-sweet gaze that accompanied it telling her all she wanted to know. The splurge was complete with the purchase of new sneakers to match the dress, then they headed for home, where, to the astonishment of Max, she changed into sweat shirt, sweatpants, and a worn pair of sneakers.

"And just what is that sexy new tennis outfit for, may I ask"—he eyed her dubiously, when she joined him in the kitchen—"if you were planning to wear this . . . ah . . . charming thing?" Amusement lurked in his gaze as he pulled at the bulkiness of the sweat shirt. Undaunted, she explained.

"The children I teach are strictly underprivileged. That tennis dress would ruin any rapport I have with them." Following Max's example, she poured herself a glass of milk.

"Then what is the outfit for?"

A spontaneous giggle erupted from her lips at

the comical look on the face before her. "Wednesday nights. I play with three women . . . for fun." A twinkle sparked her blue gaze. "We do it up big on the court," she jibed over her shoulder as she put her glass into the sink and headed for the living room. "Come on. We'll be late!" Swooping up the pile of Valentine T-shirts, she plopped them into Max's unsuspecting arms, picked up her parka and tennis racquet, and led him back out to the car.

The children adored their T-shirts almost as much as they enjoyed the sight of the tall, important-looking Max, a most patient spectator on the sidelines during their lesson. With a perceptiveness typical of children, they soon properly interpreted the attention he gave to Laura's every move; from that point on the ribbing they gave her was merciless. It was indeed a tribute to the warm rapport that they could tease her so goodheartedly.

"I like him, Laura," one child yelled at the top of her seven-year-old lungs from one end of the court to the other.

"He's watching you, Laura," declared another loudly, as though Laura weren't already acutely aware of the fact.

"Laura, you're not paying attention," one particularly sharp ten-year-old scolded in a teasing sing-song when she missed a wide shot one of the other children lobbed her way.

Through it all she parried the children's gentle barbs, and Max's obvious enjoyment of them, like the pro she was, keeping the youngsters on their toes with a steady barrage of tennis balls. It was, however, a distinct triumph when one of the boys, a precocious nine-year-old, turned the

91

tables and piped up, "Let's get him in here and see what he can do!" To the others' instant cheers and Laura's unmistakable surprise, Max did just that without batting an eyelash, grabbing an extra racquet from the pile of equipment and joining Laura on her side of the net, opposite the children.

"I thought they'd never ask," he exclaimed, no small amount of mischief written over his face. "It was getting pretty boring over there. I'm not used to being a watcher."

"I'll bet you're not!" she teased before making a pretence of turning her attention back to the children.

For a few minutes the two adults, side by side, fed balls to their fledglings. It was immediately evident to Laura that Max was no stranger to a tennis court, handling his racquet with the ease of an expert, deftly controlling the often random returns of his opponents.

Then without knowing quite how it happened, Laura found herself alone on her side of the net, with Max on the other, volleying exclusively and skillfully with her. Her class, eyes wide in excitement and pleasure, had moved to the sidelines and stood watching the actions of the duo, fascinated as though aware that something more passed between them than a tennis ball.

To Laura's pleasure Max was as strong a player as she'd competed with recently, yet she held her own unflinchingly. Even hindered as he was by his clothes which limited his freedom of movement, he easily returned every shot she hit, moving with grace and fluidity, anticipating her strategy and executing his own. The superior skill of his game brought out the best in Laura's. When they finally finished playing to the reluctant moans of their entourage, she met him at the net and, in a moment of uninhibited delight, threw her arms around his neck.

"That was terrific, Max!" she exclaimed gleefully, gasping for breath from the rigorous workout. "You didn't tell me you played tennis! And you probably haven't even built up a sweat." She kidded him, savoring the broad grin that beamed down on her.

"I don't know about that. I could use a shower right about now." He caught his breath, then turned to the children and raised both fists in an irresistible gesture of victory, Rocky-style.

True to his word he dropped Laura at her apartment and returned to his hotel to shower and change for dinner. Laura badly needed the few hours to calm her racing pulse, both from the demands of the tennis game and, more critically, from the thrill of being with Max.

As she lay on her bed fingering the gold heart at her throat, she realized that she could not remember a happier few hours. He had been helper, companion, competitor, spectator—and thoroughly at ease in each of the roles. How heavenly it would be, she mused, to spend every Saturday like this. . . .

Dinner was a continuation of the enchantment, candlelight and soft music adding to a relationship that now blossomed openly. They talked of their childhoods, their families, the day they'd just spent together. Laura felt more comfortable with him, more at home in his company, than she could have ever imagined.

"Tell me about what you do in your free time," she finally urged, yielding to the curiosity that had occupied her thoughts. "It's obvious that you play tennis," she prodded.

Max paused before answering her, drinking in the flush of excitement on her cheeks, which contributed to his own lightheadedness as much as the rosé wine before him. In the end he could not deny her. "Yes." His voice was smooth and velvet-lined. "I do play tennis. At lunchtime, several times a week at a club in Boston. Beyond that," he stated bluntly, "I lead a quiet life."

Cautiously, Laura challenged him. "I don't believe you. There's got to be *some* basis for that public image."

The arching of a dark eyebrow alerted her to the coming reprisal. "Oh, there certainly is. I am invited out by some of the most admired women in Boston. There are frequent parties at one club or another, not to mention weekends yachting around the harbor."

The voice that issued a terse, "I see," was a far cry from the one Laura had intended. This information gave her no pleasure. To her dismay a wicked smile burst forth on her date's face, accompanied by a sly chuckle. He found her displeasure amusing.

"But, you asked about my free time," he then continued calmly. "I don't consider those to be on my own time. They are business, a social necessity, and aren't especially enjoyable." Laura's eyes were held by the intensity of his, speeding her heartbeat even as it sent her a shudder of relief. Spirits suddenly elevated again, she listened, rapt, as his soothing tone flowed on.

"As for my *free* time, it really is quiet. I enjoy spending time by myself, away from the crowd. I like to read, to do crossword puzzles, even . . .

to paint." He grew almost shy, as he had once before when Laura had learned about a private and precious part of him.

"You paint?" Luminous blue eyes widened in astonishment at this latest information.

"I try. I'm not very good, I'm afraid. But it's . . . therapeutic."

Admiration overflowed both Laura's expression and her words. "I think that's wonderful! Do you do it in your town house?" she babbled excitedly, in reference to the Beacon Hill house he'd described. His offices were on the ground floor, his apartment on the second and third floors.

"No. I paint in Rockport. I have a home there. Very small. Very private. Very quiet. There isn't even a telephone."

Fascinated by the prospect of such a getaway, Laura exuded an unbridled glee that instantly justified Max's having divulged the existence of his second home. "I love it! I love it!" she exclaimed gaily. "Do you go there often?"

Pleased with her enthusiasm, he spoke freely. "Whenever I can, which, unfortunately, is not as often as I'd like. Lately"—his gaze narrowed in gentle accusation—"the Northampton Hilton seems to have become my home away from home."

Returning his tempered sarcasm, she confronted him, her blue eyes flaring in vivid contrast to her fair skin and dark hair. "There's no need for you to come out here as often as you do." Applied innocence coated the humor in her voice.

Max's brown eyes grew suddenly molten, searing her soul with its fiery bolt. "There are needs . . . and there are needs," he hedged softly. When he took her hand in his, Laura felt the burning lava flow through her veins. "I'll be going to Rockport next weekend, what with the long Washington's Birthday holiday. Will you join me, Laura?"

The lurch of excitement within her was tempered only by a lingering unsureness. The evening was divine. She felt warm, relaxed, and astoundingly happy. But a weekend with Max? It could be so wonderful . . . if she were ready for that kind of commitment.

Sensing her qualms, Max pled his case. "I'd like it very much. It would give us a chance to relax before the trial." His gaze held hers in its magnetic field as he crooned softly. "I won't pressure you; being with you would be enough." It was quite a concession for a reputed man-about-town, and Laura was as thrilled by it as she was grateful for it.

"I'd like to, Max, very much. It's just . . ." Her blue eyes clouded in the face of the conflict. For while the pulse within her thudded loudly, proclaiming her driving need to be with him, the last vestige of a principle—and a fear—prevented her unconditional acceptance.

In a gesture that endeared him to her all the more, Max reached a hand out to finger the small gold heart at her throat, the warmth of his skin replacing that where the gem had rested. "I'll call you at midweek. You have until then to decide." His patience was commendable, though the tensing of his jaw betrayed the deeper tension that her indecision caused.

Ironically, it was this very betrayal that decided the matter. At that moment Laura realized she would do anything to please Max, for in his pleasure was her own.

A smile of resolution lit her face, erasing the doubt that had hovered so tentatively about her features. "There's no need to call, Max," she vowed, a warm glow spreading through her now. "I'd *love* to go. Just tell me what to bring and how to get there!"

Five

As luck would have it, though Laura suspected that luck had little to do with it, Max was to meet with his client in Northampton on Friday afternoon, thereby allowing him to stop by for her at the end of the day and drive her the three hours east to Rockport, himself. Despite her skepticism, he also insisted that the drive back with her on Monday evening would enable him another meeting on Tuesday, and though she doubted the necessity of so many conferences— or was it the thoroughness with which he was approaching his case that disquieted her—she yielded to his determination and agreed to leave her car at home.

In the office she went through the motions of work. To say that her mind was only half in it, however, was an understatement. With skillful deflection she parried the inquisitive looks and dubious eyes that caught her daydreaming or spending long lunch hours walking through the blustery downtown streets.

Concentration seemed an elusive activity, at

least where law was concerned. Helplessly, her mind dwelt on Maxwell Kraig—his compelling personality, his rugged profile, his powerful arms, his overpowering masculinity.

The doubts she'd originally had about going to Rockport had been dismissed at the moment of her acceptance of Max's invitation. At that moment she made the commitment; there was no desire to turn back. Rather, as the weekend approached, the excitement grew, until finally early Friday evening, when her doorbell rang, she floated down the stairs to answer it with a spirit soaring on the wings of delight.

It was when she opened the door and set eyes on the boldly handsome face that smiled warmly down on her that Laura knew. She *was* in love with Max Kraig!

The shock of the discovery hit her full force. Slender, burgundy-tipped fingers clutched at the doorknob as she struggled to conceal the depth of her feelings. And once her bag had been stowed in the trunk of the Mercedes and they had begun the drive, her thoughts whirled back to this profound revelation.

The night was dark, the reflections of the headlights on the road and its wayside snowdrifts being the only source of illumination of Max's manly features, as Laura threw him the occasional sidelong glance. There was so much to consider. Where should she begin?

Her thoughts filtered back to the day she'd met him, struck by his compelling nature even in that crowded courtroom. Then later that day, he had held her spellbound, tantalizing her with a first kiss to surpass all other first kisses. From the very start she knew there was something very special about this man and his effect on her, but in her wildest dreams she never would have imagined the present developments. The level-headed, strong-willed, cool young woman she had been—and, she prayed, continued to be in other matters—she was no longer, on the matter of Max. Her emotions had managed to escape controls with which she had bound them for so long; when it came to Max, she was at the whim of a greater force.

All too clearly she recalled her stalwart practice of separating work from home. With a twinge of guilt she wondered how she could have so utterly discarded the principle. Yet she was not sorry. For in Max's company she had experienced a happiness she would have otherwise never known. Under Max's subtle influence qualities within herself had blossomed. The idea of giving, of wanting to please another above and beyond one's own feelings and needs—this she had sampled at earlier times, but never to the extent of commitment she now craved.

A car whizzed by doing far better than the 55 miles per hour Max seemed so careful to adhere to, and was soon followed by a police cruiser, lights blinking in electrical turbulence as it escorted the offender to the side of the highway.

A low-muttered "crazy driver" reached her ears as Laura's mind sped into the future. Was *she* the crazy driver here, letting her emotions carry her away at a dangerous speed? Could she help herself? No! She wanted to be here. She adored Max. And she would somehow cope with the future as it unfolded. Yet even as she willed all conflict away, the nagging in the back of her mind refused to be stilled. Even as she looked forward to the next three days, she could not deny the eerie strain of foreboding that hung in some recessed niche.

"You're awfully quiet tonight," the velvet-tongued icon of masculinity chided her gently, bringing her to the present.

"Just thinking." She gave an honest excuse, lest she be caught in a fib by the man who had a knack for doing just that.

"Then tell me about your week. Are you set to try that armed robbery?"

With an ease that was customary whenever she discussed law with Max, Laura outlined her preparations for the trial which was ten days hence. His questions were pointed, giving her a subtle suggestion here or there for her presentation. Often he made reference to one or the other of the cases he had tried himself; these stories Laura found to be both insightful and intriguing.

Time flew by in discussion, as the car left the Turnpike and headed north on Route 128 toward Rockport. She was momentarily sorry when their arrival in the town center, some forty-five minutes later, cut short their conversation, until she pinched herself with the lovely thought that they would have the entire weekend to talk. And then she caught the charm of Rockport, and all thought of talk passed from her mind.

Laura was no stranger to the North Shore, yet in its present context this oceanfront community took on an infinitely more exciting and romantic air. The streets were largely deserted on this winter's evening, a switch from the bustling summer streets she had walked on previous visits. Many of the artists' shops were closed for the winter for precisely this reason, the bulk of the tourists, the big spenders, vanishing by Columbus Day.

Now, lit by streetlights and the occasional neon-lit restaurant or shop window, the narrow streets, as Max drove slowly in deference to Laura's obvious fascination, had an ethereal quality. The snow, its frail blanket spread on lawns and curbs, was white still, an accomplishment rendered nearly obsolete by the nature and speed of traffic in most other towns. Here things moved slower. The houses, reconstructed in the style of the old fishing village, reflected the love for the quality of life that characterized the renowned artists' colony.

"This is delightful!" Laura exclaimed enthusiastically as Max pulled up to a small, quaint restaurant.

Turning in his seat to face her, he explained, tongue-in-cheek, "This is one of the few places open at this hour during the winter. The town practically folds at eight." Exaggeration that she knew it was, Laura grinned, though her reaction was more to his intense attention than to his quip. "Are you hungry?" The gleam in his eye sparkled through the darkness.

Ostensibly ignoring the implication that sent invisible waves of excitement through her, she nodded, then quickly found herself being ushered into the small eating establishment and seated at a booth toward the rear. To her surprise the owners of the family-run restaurant, as well as the attractive, blond waitress who so solicitously served them, knew him by name, and first name at that.

"Do you come here often?" Laura asked, skeptically eyeing the waitress whom Max had referred to as Gloria.

If he had intercepted her inquisitive stare, he paid it no heed. "Whenever I come out this way I make it a point to stop in. Ben and Judy have owned the place for several years now. I did legal work for them once. They're very down-to-earth, unpretentious people. I enjoy seeing them." Having loosened his tie, he looked quite rakish—five-o'clock shadow, slightly mussed hair—as he sat facing her. Although he had not changed from his business suit before they left, Laura had worn a casual pair of slacks, wool, warm, and comfortable. The prim chignon was gone, her straight black hair now flowing about her shoulders, catching the sheen of the lights as she moved her head. The cowl neck of her sweater was loose, baring enough of her slender neck to reveal the delicate gold chain and its dangling heart that she now wore constantly. It was on this necklace that Max's dazzling gaze alighted briefly, for then it followed the pink flush of pleasure that spread slowly upward from there to her cheeks.

"I'm glad you've come." His statement carried a unique force, totally different in tone from that of the sensuality his eyes conveyed. Laura could merely smile her agreement, so emotion-filled had she suddenly become. Yes, she was very glad to be here, too—even accepting that dull ache of foreboding that faintly disturbed her innermost peace.

An hour later, when Max drove up the private lane and his house came into view, she was yet more pleased to have come. For the house and its setting were breathtaking! A Cape-style structure of gray field-stone, it stood in profile as they entered the driveway, its large glass eyes staring fixedly down a snow-blotched lawn to the sea—the sea, in all its raging splendor, thrashing wildly against the dark rocks, spewing up its salt spray into geysers spearing the moonlit night. The sound could be felt even within the padded confines of the car, and as Max pulled directly into the garage beneath the house, Laura slowly exhaled the breath she'd unconsciously been holding.

"This is magnificent!" she gasped, as the automatic door slid down behind them with finality.

"Come on, let's go in," he suggested, climbing out of the car and appearing seconds later to help Laura. Laden with suitcases and briefcases, he let her unlock the doors, then directed her up a half flight of carpeted steps to a large open area which comprised the entire bottom floor of the house. Conventional it might have been on the outside, but the inside of this house was quite the opposite.

Grinning with delight, Laura flipped the light on, then made a full turn. "There aren't any *walls*. How terrific!"

Watching her closely, her host's eyes took on a gleam of satisfaction at her unbridled pleasure. "It's pretty cold here," he warned, depositing the bags by the side of the open stairs that led to the second floor. Then he headed for the thermostat. "There," he murmured aloud, "I've got the heat turned on." His dark head turned to Laura. "I'm going to build a fire. Why don't you sit down." A mischievous slash softened his lips. "I could use a cheering section." His voice was deep and sensual, sending the usual ripple of awareness her way.

He needed a cheering section like she needed a shot of adrenaline, she decided, confident that in building a blazing fire, as with all other things, he was expert. To the accompaniment of rustling newspaper, thudding logs and, finally, the gradual crackle of a nascent fire, Laura circled the entire ground level in exploration, admiring on one side of the stairway the living area with its sectional sofa in brown velvet forming a self-contained unit before the fireplace, and on the other side of the stairway the working area, desk and chairs, and the country kitchen and central eating area dominated by a heavy round pine table and four sturdy captain's chairs. With the exception of the tiled kitchen, a plush, champagne-hued carpet lay in blatant invitation to the bare-feet enthusiast.

The walls bordering the entire room bore the work of local artists. Each canvas was unique in its own way; each added to the overall feeling the room conveyed.

As she stood by the front door and looked about her, Laura was supremely conscious of the warmth and coziness—and tasteful luxury—that characterized Max's home. She wondered whether he had done the decorating himself, or whether a decorator, or some woman in his life had done it for him. Forcing the latter thought from her mind, she completed the circle, joining Max before the roaring fire as he broke from his own brooding trance to greet her.

Instantly, his expression softened, but not before she caught a glimpse of the other, more disturbed one. Yet it was past, and it, too, she willed from consciousness. A strong arm settled about her shoulders, drawing her flush beside his lean lines. His voice was thick against the black silk of her hair when he asked softly, "Do you like it?"

Mesmerized as much by the dancing flame before her as by the more predatory flame beside her, she answered his softness with her own. "You build a great fire."

Slowly, he turned her so that she faced him, his arms circling her waist, hands locking against her spine. Amusement flickered in the eyes that met hers, an amusement that curtained the more sensuous flame behind it. "Do I now?" he growled, the fingers at her back pressing her even closer against his hard body. "I'd like you to show me what kind of fire I build," he drawled. And Laura suddenly caught his gist, retaliating with a gentle pinch at his rocklike rib cage.

"That's not what I meant!" she scolded, a grin of exasperation flirting about her lips.

But Max was a step ahead of her. "And that's not what *I* meant, either. It's not the damned fire I'm talking about. Do you like the house?"

An appealing blush signaled her understanding. Nodding, she gave him the answer she felt so sincerely. "I love it, just like I knew I would. It's so . . . charming, inviting, well planned. I love it! If it were mine, I wouldn't care to leave it at all. I'd just curl up into a ball on that sofa, lay up a supply of Asti and brie, keep the fire blazing, and stay here forever . . . or until I ran out of logs," she added with a chuckle.

The sound of the laughter that serenaded her was so sweet that Laura would have continued her glowing analysis of the house, had it not been for Max's interjection. "You haven't seen the upstairs yet. You may be disappointed. You *will* find walls up there," he informed her, then went on more huskily. "But first, I've waited all evening for this."

His lips met hers, eagerly and with the masterful persuasion which was his style. Her arms wound about his waist, her hands reveling in the rippling of muscles beneath her questing touch. For a moment he drew back, lifting bold hands to frame her face then drive the length of his fingers into her hair to hold her head immobile in its tilt toward his. "I like your hair loose like this. You look very . . . touchable." His head lowered then and did touch it, his mouth covering hers with a hunger that drove all rational thought away. With reckless abandon she returned his kiss, giving herself up to the need within and the outright pleasure of the embrace.

It was Max who broke the passionate prelude, clearing his throat hoarsely as he moved back. "I have to get one or two other things from the car. Why don't you make yourself comfortable, then I'll give you the rest of the tour. You might want to see about putting on some coffee. Food will have to wait until we hit the supermarket tomorrow." By the time he had disappeared back down the stairs, she finally swallowed the lump that lingered in her throat.

The second story of the house, she discovered, was as exciting as the first. Here there were walls separating two large rooms and a bathroom. The first of the rooms, above the kitchen, was a bedroom, furnished simply but finely in shades of blue and gray to match the sea, which itself decorated practically an entire side of the room through heavy glass. The second of the rooms, that above the living room, was an airy and open studio, with a smattering of artists' tools, easels, canvases, paint tubes, set against a background of comfortable chairs and sofas. Here, too, there was a large desk and a fireplace. Glass panels similar to those in the bedroom dominated the eastern exposure, large skylights capped the ceiling. Dark as it was, Laura could only imagine the communion with the sea, indeed, with nature as a whole, that the transparency allowed.

Later, coffee cup in her hand, head resting against a sinewy shoulder, Laura was to recall her words of earlier that evening. She could stay here forever. There was a sense of peace, freedom, and warmth that permeated the house though how much of it was due to the presence of the man whose heartbeat throbbed not far from her ear, she did not know.

As the two gazed into the golden flames, a feeling of contentment floated about them, a feeling of oneness which Laura would have liked to preserve for all time. Suddenly, she wondered whether he felt the same, and the thought became all important to her. Unable to ask, she skirted the issue.

"I bet you've snowed many a lady with this little hideaway."

The hand around her shoulder tightened perceptibly on her arm as though in punishment for the prying barb. But when he met her challenge, his words took her by surprise. "You're the first."

The first? Her dark head swiveled quickly upward to view his face. He was serious. "You're pulling my leg," she quipped nonetheless, needing a moment to assimilate this information and its implication.

"I'd love to," he crooned in mischievous response to her metaphor, "but that might get a little out of hand." His arched eyebrow did not escape Laura's gaze and quickly, she looked back at the fire, determined to probe his feelings further.

"Why not? Why haven't you brought others here? Surely there must have been special women . . ." Her voice trailed off as she chided herself for her use of the past tense. Perhaps there were special women now. Perhaps she was but one of several. Somehow she sensed it was not so. His words confirmed that.

"Special women? There's only one woman who fits into that category, and she's here with me now. As I explained to you once before, Laura, this is my own very private place. And"— a catch of humor entered his velvet-smooth voice—"if I suddenly see or hear public reference to it, I'll know who's to blame." He drew her into a playful hug, which was a little too intense and lasted a few moments too long for mere playfulness. Not that Laura wasn't in a playful mood; the confession he'd just made elated her. She loved him; now he'd called her a special woman in his life. It was a start!

They sat before the fire, toasting comfortably in its warmth, engaged in easy conversation as the hours passed. They talked of the summers Laura had spent as a child at her family's summer home on Lake Champlain, where she'd discovered her proclivity for physical activity— swimming, tennis, bicycling. Max recalled more subdued times, his family life revolving around the business to the sacrifice of the type of relaxed gathering Laura had experienced.

"Is that what this house is for . . . to assure you a source of relaxation?"

"You might say that," he began hesitantly. "I believe that you have to make time for the more frivolous things. My family never did that." He paused, training his brown orbs on her blue ones. "And you know how demanding our profession can be. Did it bother you to leave everything for this weekend?" His question carried a deeper meaning than the surface words implied, and she answered it with the brightness of her eyes.

"I wouldn't have come if it had," she reasoned softly.

"Is that so?" A huskiness swelled in his throat as he lifted a hand to cup her chin, fingers caressing the gentle line of her jaw, then moving to trace her lips. Intoxicated by the muskiness that filled her senses, Laura sighed helplessly, her lips moist and parted in alluring bloom.

With a shuddering groan Max pulled her around and onto his lap as his lips accepted her invitation. Crushed against the hard firmness of his body, she surrendered completely to his masterful seduction. When his arms loosened, it was to permit them to rove more intimately over her back, her rib cage, her breasts. Instinctively, her body arched toward him, her nipples taut beneath the layers of fabric that agonizingly held his flesh from hers. Her tormented groan was a new and more heady invitation, a mindless offering from amid a mindless heaven.

Ragged breathing punctuated the deep growl by her ear as he tore his lips away abruptly. "Or is it just my body you're after, you little siren?"

Indignant, she loudly decried his allegation.

"That's absurd! I wouldn't have come just for that!"

Something had changed. The voice that now taunted her was even and astonishingly devoid of the passion that had coated it seconds before. "How do I know that? How do I know this isn't a trap?" Unable to believe her ears, or the nearly impersonal tone assailing them, she stared open-mouthed at the dark face, suddenly demonic in the fast-dying fireglow. "How do I know that you won't make demands on me once I've taken your precious virginity?" Her loud gasp was ignored as he dealt the final, insane blow. "How do I know I won't be compromised on the Stallway case?"

Hurt and infuriated, Laura's muscles mercifully held as she bolted out of his arms and away from him. "How dare you suggest such things!" she cried in frantic grappling with her madly seesawing emotions. To be so deliriously happy one minute, so distraught the next—it just wasn't fair! Striking out to conceal the pain within her, she turned, white-faced, to confront him. "You are an arrogant bastard! Do you really think your body is that irresistible? I came here for many reasons, but you wouldn't understand those." He sat in maddening relaxation, one knee crossed over the other, as he calmly bore the brunt of her tirade. It was his very composure which shattered hers. "And if you think for a minute that I intend to sacrifice my 'precious virginity' to you, you've got another thing coming, counselor." The label was a sharp reminder of their professional relationship to herself even more than to him.

Trembling legs carried her to the stairs. She grabbed the bag she had left there and climbed up to the studio, where she fully intended to spend the night.

"You're sleeping in my bed." His words were low and directly behind her. In her uproar she had not dreamed he was following her, or she would have safely slammed the door against his entrance.

Clenching her fists, she turned to him. "I'd rather burn in hell!" she seethed.

To her dismay, he grinned that anger-melting grin of his, which had reduced her to a marshmallow too often in the past. This time she vowed to resist.

"You'll neither burn in hell nor sleep on that sofa. *I* will sleep on the sofa. *You* will sleep in my bed."

"I don't want to sleep in your—"

"Keep still and get going, or I'll change my mind and take you right here on the floor." He was having fun, she marveled through her haze of fury. He thoroughly enjoyed her discomfort! Therefore, to rob him of his pleasure, she willed all anger into abeyance, raised her chin, and eyed him defiantly. Her voice, by some miracle, was cool and steady.

"Fine. I'll take your room. Since your studio means so much to you, it's all yours!" Raising both hands in a gesture of concession, she bent over to grasp her suitcase, pulling her hand away in red-hot reflex when it met his. Leaving him to carry the bag, she straightened her shoulders and crossed the hall. A moment later her suitcase was by the foot of the oversized bed and its bearer had retraced his steps to the door.

Turning to assure herself of his exit, Laura caught the raking gaze he gave her body before he left, calling softly as he closed the door, "Sleep well, tigress!"

It was a curse, nothing less! Sleep was an unreachable goal, she concluded after hours of trying. On the surface she had no complaint. The bed was firm and roomy, thoroughly comfortable, the blankets warm and enveloping, the sheets crisp against the soft fabric of her nightgown. No, what kept her awake had nothing to do with the physical conditions of her predicament. Rather, it was the psychological quagmire that deprived her of the blissful escape of sleep.

There was hurt, raw and painful, at the implications of what Max had said. Had he really thought that badly of her to imagine her harboring ulterior motives for coming here with him? It was incredible! He'd never seemed distrustful before.

There was bitter disappointment that he felt so little for her to have made such accusations. She'd had such high hopes, particularly after the things he'd said earlier. He'd seemed so sincere . . . and genuinely affectionate. Why had he suddenly lashed out at her?

Finally there was profound distress at his blatant reference to the upcoming trial, when they would have to regard each other with total indifference. There was no small amount of irony in his statement; it was not he, but Laura who had risked the most by coming away with him. It was Laura who chanced being compromised. Surely he saw that!

The early dawn hours brought with them, much as the light after the long, dark night, a certain understanding. Max had wanted to provoke her, to set her off, for some unfathomable reason. He had purposely baited her and she, fool in love that she was, had bitten—and grossly overreacted!

She firmly believed as she watched the darkness of night yield to the pale blue hues of dawn that he had not meant what he'd said. He did feel something special for her; he did trust her; he did want her here. But for some reason he had wanted, last night, to put a distance between them. Why?

All of her musings reverted to one heady possibility—that Maxwell Kraig's feelings for her were even deeper than he was ready to accept. Either he had not wanted to make love to her (and that possibility appeared remote, in light of the bold arousal she'd been keenly aware of) or he had not wanted her to give him the one thing that might imply a greater commitment, both by her and by him.

It was a mind-boggling puzzle that she grappled with. Yet the solace in the belief that there was hope for a return of the love she so deeply felt enabled her to fall, finally, into a heavy sleep, even as the first shafts of sunlight came through the window and into the room.

She awoke to the touch of a firm hand on her shoulder. The smile, relaxed and carefree, that filtered through her grogginess set the tone. If he held no grudge, neither could she. Slowly, she smiled back, inwardly pleasured at awakening to the sight of a freshly showered, denim-clad, sweatered Max.

"Forgive me?" he asked softly.

Her smile broadened, even as she reproached herself for her spineless capitulation, and she grumbled mischievously, "I seem to remember having heard that one before." Correctly interpreting her smile as a response in the affirmative, he scooped her up into his arms, then collapsed onto the edge of the bed.

"What are you doing?" she squealed in surprise.

The voice was deep, though controlled, as though he still doubted something. "Kiss and make up?"

A soft giggle slid through her lips. "You've never *asked* to kiss me before."

"I've never been such an arrogant bastard before. May I kiss you?"

Laura's blue eyes peered at him skeptically, and her voice was a saucy whisper. "Just a little one."

That was exactly what she got, to her immediate regret—a simple, light kiss on the lips, which was over before she'd even begun to be warmed. Perhaps that had been his very intention, she mused, as she found herself unceremoniously released to flip back to the pillow.

When Max made no move to leave, Laura's gaze questioned him. "Was there something else you wanted to say?"

The whiteness of his smile dazzled her. "How did you sleep?"

"Not bad." She lied, and he called her on it, noting the dark smudges shadowing each eye. Mercifully, he forced her to confess neither the extent of her poor rest nor the reason. Rather, he deftly changed the subject, inviting her to dress and come downstairs, informing her that they were going out for breakfast.

It was downhill all the way, with a return of good humor on both their sides. Breakfast was at a small shop near the ocean and was followed by a marketing expedition to buy food and drink for the weekend. It took little effort for Laura to blot out the events of the night from her mind; she was too much in love with Max to dampen his good mood. For when he was at his best, as he was on this day, he was irresistible.

The day passed in quiet relaxation. In the bright light of the sun, the house was even more cheery and open, the sea its ever-present companion, with its steadily crashing serenade. Laura spent hours by the window, looking out at the water's cold wonder. Then at Max's urging they dressed warmly and walked on the beach, hand in hand, in the most euphoric of moods.

Although Laura thought Max looked more tired than usual—and just how well had *he* slept the night before, she wondered mischievously—she dared not ask. Both avoided talk of their relationship, tacitly declaring a moratorium on any mention of affection, desire, or purpose. Increasingly, Laura found this to be the most trying. As day passed into evening, and Max served a feast of steak, salad, and wine, Laura ached to tell him of her love, so swollen had she grown with it.

The after-dinner hour found them planted once again before the fire, this time with a small distance between them, as though in open declaration that this night would be different from the last. And indeed it was.

Calmed by the wine, lulled by the soft music which sang from the stereo, hypnotized by the fire, and finally overcome by the fatigue which three hours' sleep the night before had caused, Laura curled sideways on the sofa, resting her head against it as her eyelids slowly drooped, then closed, blinding her to everything but the quiet sounds of the night, the fire, the music, the ocean, and her own most fervent dreams. It was she and Max, alone and in love, prowling the shoreline once again, hand in hand, hearts as one, their inner beauty in perfect harmony with that about them.

Suddenly, above the brush of the wind and the spray of the sea salt, warm lips touched hers in gentle cleansing, warming them from the cold of the winter air. When she awoke, the lips were there, soft against her own in tender caress.

Infinite tenderness sprang from the brown eyes that traveled about her every feature, adoration from the hands that held her hair back from her fire-flushed cheeks. "I think it's time you went to bed," he whispered. "You're exhausted."

The sound of his voice, so near and dear, brought Laura to full awareness. Suddenly, she knew exactly what she wanted. Blue eyes widening in apprehension at the thought of those hands, those eyes, those lips deserting her once more, she heard the urgent whisper, her own heartfelt plea.

"Max, don't leave me alone tonight." At that moment she wanted him more than anything else in the world. It was in part the gnawing ache in the core of her femininity that propelled her toward him; but it was also the intense psychological need to be one with this man she loved. She knew that this was indeed one of the reasons she'd come with him to Rockport. Only his total possession could satisfy the raging fires within her.

His expression had sobered beneath her plea, his dark eyes penetrating her very being. "Tell me what you want, Laura," he urged softly, his hands having fallen to the sofa on either side of her, their bodies close but no longer touching. This last was a preview of a potential hell, an emptiness she doubted she could endure.

Speaking without hesitance, her eyes luminous with a gathering moistness, she heard herself voice what she wanted above all else. "I want you to hold me, to touch me, to kiss me. I want to do the same to you. Make love to me, Max . . ." Her last words were barely audible, yet he caught every one. For an instant he hesitated, searching her depths before taking her in his arms and crushing her against his chest. Of their own accord, her hands had found their way to his brown-maned nape, clinging there with a strength born of intense longing.

There was a moment of panic when he pulled gently away from her, though his instantaneous "Shhhh" stilled her protest, as with deft movements he spread several billowing throw pillows onto the plush carpet before the fire. The resurgence of desire that flooded through her when he took her hand to ease her down to lie before the hearth was intoxicating. But Laura had no intention of being intoxicated. She was wide awake, of sound mind, and determined to experience Max's lovemaking to the fullest. It was the moment she'd waited for all her life.

Sensing her need, he overrode his own burning desire and bid his movements be slow and gentle, ever mindful of the maiden voyage this was to be. With infinite care he eased the wool sweater over her head, then, one by one, released the buttons of her shirt until it fell aside. Her bra was a simple matter, unhooked and discarded, leaving her naked beneath his gaze. When his mouth began an exploration of her flesh, she arched to meet it, the need to be touched overwhelming her.

Soft words of love, murmured low and warm against her breasts, brought their pink tips to crested peaks. Manly fingers skimmed her collarbone, her rib cage, and the deep valley connecting the two.

Driven herself by the need to explore, Laura sat up before Max and spread her hands beneath his sweater until he whipped off the offending wool, leaving his dark brown hair rakishly rumpled over his forehead. Yielding to the impulse she had to fight in times past, she combed it aside with slender fingers, shifting to her knees and lifting her mouth to taste his in turn.

Then she freed him of his shirt, savoring her first view of the manly chest which so expressed Max. Shy at first, then with growing conviction, she ran her hands over his skin, raking the soft, dark hairs as her fingertips outlined his muscular shape.

"Come here, little tigress!" he growled, suddenly impatient. As he hauled her against him, she gasped aloud at the texture of bare chest against bare breast, and her own impatience grew to explosive proportions. "If you take your things off, I can remove mine," he suggested against her hair, with a practicality inspired by pure and urgent need.

A brief moment later they stood naked before one another, lit and warmed by the graceful golden flame of the fire. Laura's eyes watched Max's as they fell from her face, to her chest, to her stomach and thighs, finally returning to the dark secret triangle that had never before been probed. When his eyes returned to hers, there was an admiration in them that fuelled the building fire within her.

"Now you look at me, Laura," he rasped. "I want you to see how much I want you, to feel how much I want you." Beneath his command she lowered her own gaze, marveling in the breadth of his shoulders, the firmness of his chest, the tapering slimness of his waist and hips . . . and the magnificent manliness that graphically interpreted his words. Unable to tear her eyes away from the boldness, she heard him utter from above her, "Touch me. Go ahead. Don't be afraid." She was in confrontation with this new and awesome force, yet she let him take her hand and guide it to himself, revealing now to her his own secrets as his other hand explored hers.

Without quite knowing how, she found herself on her back before the fireplace, his hard warm body half covering hers in sensual possession. Again and again he kissed her, his expert touch sending her to higher and higher levels of ecstasy until she cried out feverishly for release.

"Please, Max, now. Don't make me wait any longer!"

He doubted he could, even had he wanted to, so great was his own desire, sparked by this maiden's intuitively perfect responses. "Hang on to me, Laura," he crooned huskily. "We're going on a trip. The takeoff may be a little rough, but once we're off the ground, the sky's the limit. Are you with me?"

Her only answer was a breathless, "I need you, Max!"

Then the journey began. She held to him

fiercely, with but the slightest whimper of pain at the start, then, in a moment of victory, knew herself freed for all time to explore a world of passion that held untold wonders, unspoken ecstasies.

Together they explored this world, finding the tempo that bound their bodies together, growing in exquisite harmony with one another, soaring higher and higher until the peak of delight was reached, at last, exploding into a downpour of brilliant firebursts and starlit sensations.

It was much later, when the fires had faded to glowing embers, that Max carried Laura upstairs to his bed, placing her gently on one side while he climbed in on the other.

"Don't leave me," she begged in a startled whisper, turning to face Max, stretching her arms out to touch him, refusing to relinquish the mind-shattering wholeness she had newly discovered.

"I won't, baby, I won't." He soothed her, drawing her once more against the warmth of his body, tucking her curves neatly into his own contours, imprisoning her within the steel bars of his arms.

In very much the same posture of intimate communication, they awoke the next morning, both having succumbed to the numbed sleep of the satisfied lover. In the brightly sunlit morning, he took her again, his unbounded gentleness easing her through the lingering soreness to another spiraling peak. When she cried out at the moment of heavenly release, it was as much at the tremors that shook Max's spasming body as at her own pulsing joy.

The experience was to be repeated over again throughout their stay, with each interlude fuelling, rather than sating, each zenith surpassing its predecessor. The only blotch on the beauty of their affair was the knowledge that Monday night would see them back to Northampton— back to business and separate sides of the courtroom.

Their last few hours were spent walking the streets of Rockport, admiring the canvases and the sculpture, examining the handiwork of the other arts. Together they dined on fish chowder and old-fashioned strawberry shortcake, wearing it off on a long, final walk on the cool beach.

As the Mercedes headed back toward the highway, a heavy silence fell between them. To Laura it was a strange paradox that crystalized. For as long as she could remember she had put her professional life first, refusing to allow her personal life to interfere. Now the tables had been turned. For the first time in her memory she had found a true and total happiness, a genuine and thorough relaxation, an absolute and utter fulfillment. This was what Max had given her; this was all woman. But how to reconcile lawyer with this other, more vulnerable yet infinitely rewarding role—that was the dilemma. Yes, for the first time in her twenty-eight years, it was the professional life that threatened to interfere with the personal life. In the matter of Maxwell Kraig, her personal life now took precedence. And it was with near resentment that she contemplated the necessity of her return to work.

Six

Her only consolation as she returned Max's final, heart-rending hug on her doorstep late Monday night was that he was as disturbed as she.

"Why don't you stay the night here?" she suggested impulsively, even though she knew that he could not.

He shook his head, the strong arm around her softening his grimace. "As it is, we have a problem here of conflict of interest. And I don't know how in the hell we're going to resolve it!" She agreed wholeheartedly.

Hedging softly, she tried to lighten the prospect. "There is still a little over a month until the trial. Something will come up."

"I hope so, baby. I hope so." Then, with a final and surprisingly gentle kiss, he left, the imprint of his lips on hers her only saving grace through the desperately lonely night.

There was one other mind-diverting incident on that same night. The softly hissing steam had barely begun its journey through the radiators when the peal of the telephone tore through the emptiness which enveloped her.

"Laura! Finally! Where have you been?" It took her several seconds to recognize the mildly agitated sound as the voice of Franklin Potter.

"Frank? I've been away. Is something wrong?" A shaft of fear stabbed at her, the thought that perhaps her father was ill.

"No, everything is all right . . . now that we've

located you." Laura could picture the ruddy, rounded cheeks puffing as the voice scolded on. "But your father has been frantic. He's been trying to reach you since Saturday morning. Where have you been?"

In no mood to divulge her most precious secret, she hedged. "I'm sorry. I was away. Was it something urgent he wanted?"

Frank sighed in resignation. "Why don't you give him a ring and find out, my dear. It's still early enough out there, but I'm going to sleep. I'll see you tomorrow morning, Laura."

After gently bidding her protector good night, Laura phoned her father, only to discover that the "emergency" was a conference he'd wangled an invitation to in Hartford around the time of the Stallway trial. Victoriously, he informed her he'd be able to make the short trip from there to Northampton for a day or two to watch her performance. And, despite the gnawing in the pit of her stomach at the thought of the trial, Laura felt true pleasure that he would be there. She would need all the moral support she could get!

"Please apologize to Frank for me. When I couldn't get you on the phone after twenty-four hours, I got worried. A father's prerogative, sweetheart! Where were you anyway?"

There it was, the same innocently piercing question coming to haunt her from two different sources—and she'd barely taken off her coat and sorted through Saturday's mail! "I was away for the weekend. You know, the holiday and all . . ."

Mercifully, her father didn't pursue the matter. "Well, I hope you had a good time. Next time, leave word with someone, okay?"

Next time. Would there be a next time? Of

course. There had to be! As Laura hung up the telephone, she wondered what would happen next, in this most unexpected and impractical of love affairs. Max had promised he would stop by the office after his meeting with Jonathan Stallway; she had that to look forward to. As for the rest, her bed was a cold and barren wasteland when she finally tumbled into it.

Her thoughts centered on the memory of Max's warm, hard body close to hers, as it had been for the past two nights. All too easily she could become addicted to his nearness; even now, its absence gnawed at her insides. Yet, as she lay alone in her bed, she was able to look back on the weekend with a clarity his very nearness had prevented.

How strange it was—her body had been forever altered, yet she could not now imagine it otherwise. She had lost her virginity to the man she loved. There were no regrets. It had happened as naturally as spring's awakening follows winter's sleep. Whereas her initial attraction to Max may have been physical, it had developed into so much more that she honestly believed, both of herself and of him, that the weekend had been conceived for the very companionship each would give the other. Its consummation had been an inevitable link in the chain of events which was their steadily blossoming relationship.

Now as her hand skimmed the swells and hollows of her own body, brought to full womanhood by the fullness of this man, Laura sensed that Max would be her first, last, and only lover.

The following morning she was at her desk, the efficient prosecutor, hair pulled back into a tidy twist, dressed as conservatively as ever, dark head bent over her papers in an all-out attempt at self-discipline, when Max stopped in. Only he knew the cause of the pink flowering on her cheeks. Only she knew the cause of the involuntary quivering the sight of the tall, brown-haired, brown-eyed counselor generated.

They talked for a few brief moments, Max perched on the desk at the corner nearest her, when it came time for him to head back to Boston. The dark gaze darted mischievously to the door for clearance before his head lowered to kiss her ever so gently on the cheek. Both knew the chaste peck to be totally inadequate. Instinctively, Laura turned her head just enough to meet his waiting lips, surrendering fully to their pressure, then demanding on her own that little extra that would have to tide her over until she saw him again. It was this mutual hunger, unfortunately, that nearly snatched their newborn affair from the ranks of the clandestine.

The clearing of a throat, conspicuous as it had been on another occasion, drew both heads with a start toward the door. There Frank Potter stood, hands on hips, entering the room only when he was certain that the business he'd interrupted was over.

"I hope I'm not disturbing anything," he snorted with a smirk that did not match the sobriety behind his wire-rimmed spectacles. Then, as was his manner, he went on without awaiting a response, his eyes traveling from one to the other before settling finally on Laura. "Did you get through to your dad?"

Fully aware of the burning of her cheeks, she chose to ignore her embarrassment, instead willing her voice to be calm and even. "Yes, thanks, Frank. It was nothing important. He apologized for disturbing you."

"No need for apology," Frank snapped back quickly, sending a dubious look toward Max, who now stood off to the side. Then Frank added, "I was as worried. I'd never forgive myself if something happened to my favorite lawyer while she's under my protection." His words were pointed, as was the warning in the eyes that shifted from face to face again before he nodded his departure. "Laura, Max . . ."

Only when the doorway was once more free of his portly presence did Laura turn to her partner in deception. "That was just lovely." She spoke with soft sarcasm. "It seems I've got an army of watchdogs around here." Quickly, she explained about the previous evening's calls. Max was neither amused nor relieved, his face taking on a grim set as his mind had moved a step ahead. He was seriously concerned about the pressure she might receive should their relationship become known. Unfortunately, she misinterpreted his intention.

"I think we'd better cool it a bit, Laura," he suggested hesitantly. "That was too close for comfort. I'll phone you toward the end of the week. Okay?" As always, he was in total control of himself, something Laura was far from. Rather, her thoughts tripped clumsily over one another. Was he ashamed of their involvement? Was he letting her down easily? Had it meant nothing at all to him, aside from a simple "I'll phone you toward the end of the week"?

Max honed in on her hurt immediately. "Don't look at me like that, little tigress," he growled, astounding her with his switch to the near-playful. "I've got to get back to work and so do you." Then his voice deepened. "Please trust me. Everything will work out just fine." He was once again the caring lover, his gaze warm, his smile genuine, his words confident—all throwing Laura into a well of even greater confusion. One instant she was sure he was kissing her goodbye, the next, merely adieu. Which was it?

This time it was the strong fingers that touched his own lips to carry his kiss to hers, lingering for a fraction of a moment to caress the soft curve of her mouth, before withdrawing. Misted blue eyes watched him leave, the tightness in her throat mercifully preventing her from saying the words that cried from within for expression. *I love you, Maxwell Kraig,* she whispered finally, then lowered unseeing eyes to her work.

The week slid by on a seesaw as Laura's emotions fluctuated wildly, joy-filled and high at times, empty and heart-torn at others. At midweek she was at one of the lower points, convinced that her love was ill-fated, when the D.A. called her into his office. He was, as always, the ultimate diplomat, discussing several timely matters of law with her before throwing in the corker.

"Is Kraig giving you a hard time?"

Laura had expected his inquisition sooner, on Monday or Tuesday, and when it hadn't come, she had slipped into a state of complacency. Now she was shaken by his sudden reference to the incident he had witnessed. And his words could not have been more appropriate. Max certainly was giving her a hard time. She was madly in love with him; thoughts of him monopolized her mind. Yes, he *was* giving her a hard time!

"No, of course not!" She lied, a cynical twist to her lips the only evidence of her inner state.

His head lowered as he stared at her over his glasses, reminding Laura of the stereotypical family doctor. The conjured image was a blessing, for it brought a more relaxed smile to her face, enabling her to answer the D.A.'s persistent "Are you sure?" with a more confident ring.

"Yes, Frank, I'm sure. Actually, I've learned a lot from him," she began, then hurried on, mortified by her own words. "He's a brilliant lawyer. Has he decided to try the Wilkins Home case?" she asked innocently.

"I believe he has, but then, you knew that, didn't you, Laura?" he chided. He could be diplomatic, and he could be blunt. This was a case of the latter. But, as always with his "favorite lawyer," he did not let her squirm for very long. "Look, honey, this is your affair." She winced at the term he'd coincidentally chosen. "But I just want you to keep your eyes open. A passing kiss or two, an evening out with the man may be all right. But watch out for anything more. You could be hurt, personally *and* professionally."

It was the second such warning Frank had given her, and coming at this particular time, when it seemed an eternity since she'd spoken to Max, she wondered whether he was right. The weight of uncertainty pained her, the pressure of a love bottled up becoming more and more oppressive. Was this just a preview of the future?

The time stretched out, made infinitely worse by an inordinate number of phone calls where the caller had chosen either to be still and listen to her intermittent hellos or hang up, until Friday night, when the telephone finally rang once more.

128

"Hello?" she answered timidly, terrified that it would be another false alarm. It was not.

The deep growl, strangely excited, vibrated across the miles directly to her heart. "Hello, yourself! How are you, Laura?"

"Great!" *Now,* she added silently. "How about you?"

"Now that I hear your voice, much better." Well, she thought ruefully, he was more forthright than she had been. Or was it merely a much-practiced line he'd delivered?

"B-busy week?" she stammered unsurely.

The velvet tone had an instant soothing effect on her. "Yes, it's been busy. But worse, it's been very lonely. I've missed you, Laura!"

Any doubt of his sincerity was cast to the wind, fallen victim both to his urgent words and the sheer joy of hearing from him. "Same here, Max," she murmured shyly. "I was beginning to think you'd forgotten me." Subconsciously, she fingered the small gold heart, a habit that had given her solace during the week.

"You know better than that," he chided gently. "Are you ready to go for Monday?" His reference was to the armed robbery case they'd discussed at length.

"Uh-huh. I've got a little work to do, but otherwise we're all set." With great care, she covered herself; she could easily busy herself or she could as easily manage to be free, should he decide to come to Northampton.

The conversation continued on an impersonal vein, warm yet noncommittal, until Max finally drew it to a close. "Good luck on Monday, Laura. I'll be anxious to hear the verdict. How long do you expect the trial to last?"

With no mention yet of his seeing her, Laura strove to conceal her disappointment. "Several days at least. I doubt it will make the Boston papers, though," she put in as an afterthought. If he wanted to know the outcome, he'd just *have* to call her, she vowed rebelliously.

Max answered her with maddening sureness. "Oh, I have my spies at work for that sort of thing," he chuckled, his humor escaping her. "And don't work *too* hard, little tigress. Got that? I'll do enough extra work this week for the two of us."

Puzzled, she prodded, "You're not on trial, are you?" He had mentioned nothing of a particularly heavy week ahead.

The sensuous timbre quickened her pulse, as he explained. "No, I'm not on trial, but I sure as hell had better find something to keep my mind off *you*. I have a feeling it's going to be another trying week." Laura laughed aloud at his pun, tickled by his sentiment.

"You're impossible," she scolded through a lingering chuckle.

"So you keep telling me." The deep drawl sizzled over the line. "Be good, baby. I'll be thinking of you."

Small consolation that was; in place of his big, bold presence she must settle for his long-distance thoughts! "Thanks, Max. Bye-bye." She bit her lip, once again swallowing the more meaningful words that pride prevented her from voicing. Was it pride? Fear? Or both? Whatever, it was a moot point. The line was dead, the connection severed. Once more Laura was left nothing but her memory, her love, and the hollow deep within.

Taking a dose of Max's own medicine, she threw herself headlong into the last-minute preparations for the trial. It didn't help that when she took time out to teach her tennis class Saturday the children barraged her with questions about her "man"—where was he, was he coming again, would she ask him? Nor did it help that Mrs. Daniels threw in her own little jab about Laura not being as hardy to carry her bundles as her "beau" had been.

By the time Monday morning rolled agonizingly around, the prosecutor was, if anything, over-prepared for her case, albeit under-rested. Concealer had sufficiently covered the darkness beneath her eyes, such that she was the image of composure and competence, when the trial began. Once the business of selecting a jury had successfully brought on the opening arguments, she found herself totally engrossed in the legal process, as clear-headed before the judge, as skillful before the witnesses, as effective before the jury as her reputation promised. As always when she was on trial, she returned home at night in a state of exhaustion, mustering only enough strength to review her notes for the coming day before falling into bed. It was in many ways a blessing, this all-consuming fatigue, for she was left with precious few moments to ponder Maxwell Kraig.

In fact her only distractions during these evening crash sessions were the phone calls that tore through the silence once or twice each night, sometimes from a friend inquiring as to the progress of her case, sometimes from the silent caller whose persistence had begun to annoy her . . . but never from Max.

So successful was the diversion of the trial from her personal quandary that she was almost sorry when, on Thursday afternoon, the jury returned with its verdict, thankfully in her favor, guilty on all counts. The sentencing date was set, the jury excused, and Laura returned to her office amid hearty congratulations from her colleagues, the office staff, and the D.A. himself. But nothing from Max.

Pondering the exact nature of the spies he'd mentioned, she returned to her apartment. But the only call that came over the five hours before she finally succumbed to exhaustion, was the wordless one, disturbing her an infuriating two times with his rings, then silence. It crossed her mind to report this pest to the telephone company, yet she knew it was probably a prankster who would never be caught. During the second of the calls, when fatigue had taken claim of any good humor she might have had, she impulsively launched an indignant tirade, then hung up in even greater fury when her harsh words brought nothing more than a faint "tsk, tsk."

It was Friday morning when, cross as a bear, she stomped down to answer the doorbell and was handed the instantly recognizable yellow envelope of a telegram. Sure enough, it was from Max.

DEEPEST CONGRATULATIONS ON
YOUR SUCCESS. AM PROUD OF YOU.

MAX

Was that it, she asked herself in disbelief. Was that all he had to say? No phone call, just this two-sentence bit of impersonal garbage?

Fighting the hurt that threatened to reduce her

132

to tears, she carefully folded the telegram and replaced it in its envelope, stashing it in a bureau drawer, out of sight but accessible, before she headed for the office.

Swamped in disappointment, aching from the seeming inadequacy of his response, Laura quickly took care of any office business that had piled up during the trial, then bundled herself up, packed her briefcase, and took off for the rest of the day, knowing the mini-holiday to be well earned, what with the hours she'd kept while on trial.

The afternoon and evening found her at home, waiting in vain for a very particular phone call. As the hours passed, self-doubt flared. Had she imagined the warmth he held for her? Had she, in her cocoon of love, misread his actions? Had she, having given this man the very treasured part of her that was no more, been merely viewing their relationship through rose-colored glasses? Why hadn't he called?

Question after question arose, to be reiterated mere moments later. Hadn't Max realized how important each trial meant to her? Wouldn't he have wanted to congratulate her in person, or, at least, over the phone? How wonderful it would have been to hear his voice.

Hurt and bewilderment gave way to anger. Who was he to keep her on tenterhooks like this? Well, she was not about to sit around forever awaiting word from him—and she was getting tired of the other phone calls, those nuisance ones that had continued to plague her. It was nine o'clock when, in a fit of frustration, she took the phone off its hook and let it dangle freely toward the floor. There. Now she would not be expecting either call!

All night the phone remained uncradled. All night her anger remained intense, unabated by the passage of time and the coming of a new day. If anything, she was even more annoyed that with Saturday morning there was still no sign of Max. Why she had expected him to show up at her door, she didn't know; it was wishful thinking that seemed destined to remain unfulfilled.

Slamming the telephone receiver back in its proper place, she vowed to keep herself busy all day. Several phone calls later, she set out to do just that, intermixing her shopping and tennis class with lunch out and then, much later, a visit and dinner with friends. It was good to see the Davissons, a couple to whom she had grown quite close since she'd arrived in Northampton three years ago. Amanda had been a classmate of hers at Mount Holyoke and had married Mark right after graduation, while Laura had gone on to law school. Now Amanda and Mark were the proud and busy parents of a six-month-old, and tied as they were to the house more than they'd been in the past, Laura was a frequent and welcome visitor. She merely had to phone and say she was on her way, and the door was opened to her.

Always before, Laura had enjoyed these visits, enthusiastically conversing with her friends, while all three cooed over the baby. This particular Saturday night was different however.

Amanda and Mark were obviously very much in love with each other, and as obviously crazy about the baby. Laura found herself imagining that it was she and Max who were married so happily, fussing over a brown-mopped, brown-eyed child who squirmed before them. It was an image charged with poignant beauty, staying with her when she thanked her friends and took her leave to reluctantly return to the loneliness of her apartment. The image began to crack when she found no sign of any attempted contact by Max—no note on the door, no mail, no second telegram, no message with Mrs. Daniels. But her loneliness dissolved when, a short time later, she turned on the television to watch the late news. The first items dealt with labor difficulties, an all-too-frequent and totally political problem in the state. A part of Laura tuned out impatiently. The next item, however, drew her full and fervent attention.

The familiar-faced anchorman eyed the camera somberly. "An investigation has begun into the death of ten-year-old Larry Porotska, a resident of the Wilkins Home for Retarded Children." Laura's horror grew as the man continued. "The severely handicapped child, a six-year resident of the Home, was found dead in his bed early this morning. Angry parents, including those of the deceased, thronged the administration building to demand an inquiry into the cause of the child's death. This tragic incident occurs close on the heels of the filing of complaints by a group of these same parents charging negligence at the institution. Earlier this evening our on-the-scene reporter, Mary Hall, was able to speak with Boston attorney, Maxwell Kraig"—Laura's pulse began to race as her eyes remained glued to the set—"who will represent the parents in this class-action suit."

The camera switched to the footage that had Laura trembling in anticipation. There, framed by the chrome and wood edging of her television set, was the face of the man she loved. The camera

135

zoomed in on him as the reporter sought his comments.

The deeply confident voice Laura knew so well came loud and clear over the air waves, "There will be an autopsy performed on the body of the child. Until those results are made known, I have no comment." Sitting on the edge of her seat, dwelling on his every word, Laura cheered him on in the constant battle against prejudicial pre-trial publicity. Despite the urgings of the quick-witted reporter, he was not about to be trapped. Twice more, she baited him, cleverly rewording the same questions. Twice more, he successfully evaded making a commitment. Sensing that there would be no intimate insights from this lawyer, the camera moved back to afford a longer shot. At this moment Laura caught her breath.

Max had obviously been stopped on his way out for the evening. His dress was formal and immaculate, his dark tuxedo visible beneath his overcoat, a white scarf dashingly setting off the combination. He looked freshly shaven, carefully groomed, and perfectly at ease before the cameras. As they pulled back farther, Laura tried in vain to identify the location. She had no trouble, however, recognizing the stunning blonde not far from his elbow as Sara Beth Wilson, an outspoken theater critic for a competing television station, presumably the reason why the camera had avoided her. Now Laura froze as she heard Mary Hall thank Max for his time, closing her report with a devastating, "We hope we haven't made you and Miss Wilson late for tonight's opening at the Colonial. Enjoy yourselves and thank you. And now back to our anchor desk . . ."

With a bound Laura whammed the off switch of the television. She had seen enough. There had been Max, on the way to the theater no less, with . . . with . . . a renowned beauty! Here she was, pining away for him! No wonder she hadn't heard from him!

If she had been depressed earlier, it was the black pit of despair in which she now found herself. She had been so foolish, assuming that Max returned even half of her feelings! How wrong she'd been . . . how tragically wrong!

The shrill sound of the telephone physically jolted her. Laura saw red; if it was Max calling at this late hour, having spent a full evening with the blond bombshell of the airwaves, she would give him a piece of her mind. Clenching her teeth, she stormed into the kitchen and snatched up the receiver.

"Hello!" she yelled into a subsequent and continuous silence. *Oh, God, not again!* She sighed, then repeated her command. "Hello!" Silence. As she readied to hang up on the perverted phoner, a new sound caught her attention and promptly appalled her. Heavy breathing, vulgar and obscene in its wordless implication. With a shudder of revulsion she slammed down the receiver. It was the last straw!

Racked by a gamut of emotions ranging from sorrow, pain, and heartache, through jealousy, hurt, and puzzlement, to disgust and finally, fear, she surrendered to the storm of long-pent-up tears, throwing herself across her bed in utter defeat. It was in this position that she cried herself to sleep, the first time she had done so since she'd been a child.

But Sunday dawned a new day, and as far as

Laura was concerned, a new start. Gone were the hopes of Max's calling her. Dispelled were the dreams of his loving her. All that remained was the ache of a love which was not to be. Unable to fault him for something he'd never claimed, Laura had only herself to blame. He had never spoken of love; he'd never made promises he hadn't kept. It had all been in her own wild fantasies.

There was a bitter irony in Max's performance last night, she mused sadly. Just as he had refused to take a stand on the death at the Wilkins Home, parrying the reporter's hints with ease, so he had, she now saw in hindsight, refused to take a stand on his feelings toward her.

Determined to work Maxwell Kraig out of her system, Laura dressed, drank a cup of coffee quickly, and headed for the library to bury herself amid her silent and steady hardbound buddies.

Last night's phone call suddenly hit her with new force. In her agony over what she had seen on TV she had blotted out that very call that had finally broken her. Who was calling her? Why? Was it a mere prankster . . . or something more? Perhaps it was time to report these incidents.

But many people receive crank calls. If she persisted in ignoring them, surely the perpetrator would grow bored. Her reaction last night had been to the sight of Max on television with another woman. For the time being, she vowed to stay calm and hang up the phone when the nuisance calls came. But heavy breathing—was that pure nonsense?

She worked feverishly through the day. When she finally returned home at eight thirty, the telephone was the first sound to greet her. Her

138

stomach began to jump. Should she let it ring or answer it? Let it ring, let it ring, one part of her cried, wishing only to avoid confrontation with either Max or the prankster. Answer it now, the other part argued, suggesting that it could be her father, a friend, or a work-related call. In any case she should not be made a fugitive in her own home. This latter voice won out. Gingerly, she put her hand to the receiver; timidly, she raised it to her ear. Then she waited and listened. The wait was short.

"Hello? Laura?" Pause. "Laura? Are you there?" Perversely wishing she'd decided not to answer even as her pulse raced in involuntary excitement, she heard Max's voice, loud, clear, and quite concerned. "Hello? Laura!"

"Hello, Max," she responded quietly.

"Is something wrong, Laura?" He *was* concerned.

"No, no. I'm just tired—"

"I've been trying to get you all day. Where have you been?" It was none of his business where she'd been; she hadn't asked where *he'd* been. Yet why did he sound so worried?

In a faltering voice she began. "I've been . . . busy . . . working."

"Working? All weekend?"

Gradually her composure grew. "No, I haven't been working *all* weekend." Let him think what he wished, she mused spitefully.

"Laura, is everything all right?" His voice was softer, more gentle now, quickly approaching the melting point. Realizing this, she steeled herself for its heat, willing her voice to remain as cool as possible.

"Of course. Everything is fine." She lied.

"You don't sound right." How perceptive of him, she acknowledged with a sigh. A silence followed his accusation, during which she felt at a total loss. Her greatest urge was to tell him how she missed him, how she wanted him. Yet even this made her angry. Finally she took a deep breath.

"Was there something you wanted?"

Again a silence, as though Max were unsure himself. "Did you get my telegram?"

"Yes. Thank you." Another silence.

The force of his explosion made her jump. "Look, Laura, I don't know what's going on, but I don't like it. I'm going to be in on Friday and I'd like to see you that evening. Do you think you could make dinner? I'd like to talk in private."

Under the burden of confusion Laura's eyes brimmed liquid. Just this morning she'd willed this compelling man out of her life. Now the very sound of his voice was enough to make her rethink her vows. Maybe he would have some explanation for her. Maybe they would be able to straighten things out. . . .

"Laura?"

Her voice was a mere whisper. "Yes, Max, that's fine."

Suddenly, there was the deepest tenderness, almost a pain in his voice. "What is it, baby?" His tone, his words, the fact that he was finally on the other end of the line choked her and made her incapable of speech. "Laura, I'm driving out there now—"

"No!" she cried out frantically, then quieted. "No, Max. I'm perfectly all right. Just tired. I'll see you on Friday."

Despite her efforts to push it out of memory,

the low croon she heard was forever imprinted on her mind. "Laura, I . . . miss you. I'll see you then."

Not knowing if she felt better or worse, she cradled the receiver, made herself a cup of hot chocolate with two marshmallows on top, and curled up on the sofa. It took little thought for her to realize one stark fact. She wanted so badly to see and be with Max that she would forgive him most anything . . . as long as he came back to her! Love was such a complex emotion, so overpowering and all-consuming. Love conquered all, the old saying went. In her case it was true. The anger, the hurt, the bitterness—all had simply evaporated the minute she'd heard his voice. If only Max could feel the same.

The phone rang once again that evening, the earlier debate renewed, ending similarly. This time it was Frank, calling to ask about one of her other cases. Although she could have sworn she had discussed the very matter with him before, she chalked her confusion up to the pressure she'd been under. She had no way of knowing that the D.A.'s call was purely one of concern, sparked by an unexpected call he himself had received moments earlier.

The anticipation of seeing Max kept her buoyed up all week. She willed any negative thoughts into the background. Even the few repeated incidents of heavy breathing seemed less crucial, and as she had decided, she calmly and quickly replaced the receiver on each of these occasions.

Friday couldn't have come soon enough. To avoid a possible meeting with Max in the courthouse, Laura left work early, questioning whether she would be able to remain neutral to Max in a public place. *My God,* she found herself wondering, *if I am so concerned about a simple encounter here, how am I ever going to manage the trial?* The only conclusion she reached, as she whipped up egg whites for a soufflé, was that it was the *personal* nature of this particular encounter that was throwing her; in an impersonal professional situation, she vowed, she would be able to keep her cool. And with the trial less than three weeks off, she prayed this would be the case.

Seven

Never had Laura taken such care dressing. After lengthy deliberation, she chose a pair of soft wool slacks, snug-waisted and slim-hipped, with a matching hand-knit sweater. Her hair fell free, her cheeks flushed slightly, her beautifully manicured nails in vivid contrast to the paleness of her skin. Those slender hands were none too steady when the doorbell rang; reflexively, she touched the small gold heart, rubbing its ruby nervously.

She opened the front door to reveal a Maxwell Kraig even more mighty and attractive than he'd been before. His face was the proverbial oasis in the desert, the merciful return of the dove to the Ark. Awestruck by the torrent of emotion that washed over her, she silently stood aside to let him enter, closed the door behind him, then looked almost shyly up at the face that beheld hers. His expression was serious, his gaze intense, his mouth betraying a tension that seemed gradually to abate as they looked at one another.

"Hey . . ." he whispered in a husky greeting that demanded but one in return. In a split second Laura was in his arms, heedless of the chill that lingered on his heavy jacket, conscious only of the bulk that held her to him. Eager lips came together in hungry fusion, a mutual excitement emanating from the embrace.

Reluctantly, Max finally drew back, holding Laura at arms' length to study her features. "How are you, baby?" he crooned deeply, drawing a slow but steady smile of happiness to Laura's glossy lips. Nothing had changed—not the warmth of his eyes, nor the strength of his smile, nor the tenderness of his hands, nor the very essence of masculinity that so entrapped her. Regardless of what had happened since she'd been with him in Rockport, he was just the same and she loved him dearly.

Sensing that some crisis had been resolved in his favor, he swung her around beside him, an arm across her shoulders, guiding her upstairs to the living room. Laura had not yet spoken; with Max, communication took a different form. Her insides jangled with excitement as he shed the sheepskin jacket and turned to face her. He smelled newly showered and shaved—that clean smell that she adored tantalizing her. His gray slacks were finely complemented by a heavy wool sweater, which added even greater breadth to his shoulders as its dark, charcoal shade gave him an air of mystery.

Laura was only marginally aware of Max's corresponding assessment of her, so occupied was she drinking in his phenomenally good looks. He, however, was fully cognizant of her examination—and pleased by it. A broad smile flashed white and wicked across his face in wordless teasing. Then he spoke, deep and sonorously.

"I was worried about you. Are you all right, Laura?"

Once before she had cut short her response to this question. This time she gave full vent to her love. "I am now," she murmured softly, her eyes willingly drowning in his.

She heard his groan, a low sound akin to a marathoner's agonized exhalation at victory, then she was hauled against his chest in a hug so fierce her breath was stolen. "God, how I've wanted you," he growled against her hair, moments before possessing her lips with his searching mouth. Laura gave to him all he asked, and when she found herself a short time later in her bedroom, being undressed slowly and sensually by her lover, she could have imagined no other course of events.

If their first adventure in lovemaking had been driven by an intractable hunger, this night's coupling was to be one of mutual exaltation. As they lay atop fresh pink sheets, Max's dark body in sharp contrast to Laura's soft, creamy one, they explored their very differences—feeling, seeing, tasting in near worshipful admiration. As hungry as each was, the need went deeper than pure lust and its physical gratification.

Laura urged Max on with soft words of encouragement, overcoming all inhibitions beneath his masterful tutelage, growing increasingly confident both of her right to enjoy the pleasures of his manhood and of her ability to pleasure him with her womanhood. He coaxed her on with words of passion as his ardor mounted, his excitement enhanced by the knowledge that she was eager and ready to receive him. When he moved between her thighs and they were finally one, she gasped aloud at the beauty of the union, marveling that anything could be so very precious. Indeed, it was to be a night for marveling, as he took her to height after height of orgasmic ecstasy, each more profound than the one before.

Dinner was late, rock Cornish hens and spinach soufflé taking a back seat to this more pressing, non-culinary delight. So divine was his company, as he insisted on hearing every detail of the armed robbery case she'd tried, then filled her in on the facts of the Wilkins Home case, that Laura forgot the woman she'd seen with Max on television, even the purgatory of uncertainty in which she'd spent too much of the past two weeks. The only thing of import was that he was with her now.

However, he did confront her about the phone call he'd made to her the previous Sunday night. "What was that all about?" he asked pointedly, his dark eyebrows lowering in concern. "You sounded strange, as though you were frightened."

Impulsively, she blurted out the truth, in search of comfort from this man who held the key to it. "I was—I mean, not really frightened—but hesitant. I've been getting crank calls, and thought that might just be another."

"What kind of calls? What does the caller say?" he prodded gently, listening soberly as she recounted the history of the calls. "Heavy breathing? No words at all?"

"Nothing! I've never heard a voice. The caller may be either male or female, young or old. I have no hint whatsoever. But"—she chided herself aloud—"I've made a big deal out of nothing. It's annoying, that's all. I'm sure there's no real problem."

Max pacified her. "You're probably right." His expression, however, mirrored the same uneasiness she felt. "Let's watch it a little longer and see if anything changes. Then, if necessary, we can put a tap on your phone to record and trace the source of the call."

"Oh, Max," she protested feebly, "I'm sure it's nothing!"

"I hope so," he echoed, more skeptically than she might have wished.

That night Laura slept within the protective circle of Max's arms, curled against his leanly masculine shape, their legs intertwining. He had given her a token, wickedly mischievous argument when she'd insisted he stay the night, but her possessiveness pleased him.

To her utter delight he was to spend the whole weekend in Northampton, working with his client in the county jail while she went about her usual Saturday business, then meeting her back at her apartment later in the day. Ironically, the phone did not ring once.

"Hmmm . . . no calls while *you're* here. Maybe *you're* the one who's been terrorizing me," she quipped impishly.

He saw no humor in her words. "Sometimes you are a little too smart for your own good," he said, angry. "You take this as a huge joke, I find

146

it disturbing." The flashing in his eyes eased immediately upon seeing Laura's distress.

It was a begrudging "Sorry I mentioned it" that slid through her lips. But there was a fine thread of tension that penetrated their remaining time together.

Laura suspected that the business of the crank calls had little to do with the real source of the tension. Rather it was their own relationship and the fact that they would have to come to grips with it in some form before the start of the Stallway trial, two weeks from Monday.

Additionally, as much as Laura fought its intrusion on the time they did have together, there was the constant knowledge that this weekend was only that, and would be over much too soon. Whether Max's occasional remoteness stemmed from the same source, she didn't know. But intermittent distraction there was, on both sides, and it was not to be easily dismissed.

Bacon and eggs were frying noisily late Sunday morning when the phone rang. Laura reached for a dishtowel to wipe her hands and answered it, fully expecting the booming voice of her father, stunned to hear the wretchedly exaggerated breathing that so repulsed her. Instantly she hung up.

A sharp glance up caught Max at the door of the kitchen, wearing only snug denims. "Same thing? Just heavy breathing?" Quite accurately he had interpreted her pallor and the hardening of otherwise gentle features. He read her well, she mused ruefully, merely nodding her head.

The squared jaw was even more sharply defined when she darted a second glance at him. "Laura," he began, coming to stand closer by her side, "I think we should report—" only to be cut off.

"No, Max! There's no need. I'd feel like a fool making a major issue out of it." The actual concern in her own eyes was hidden from his view as she drained the bacon onto some paper towels.

"Why not just change your number? Very simple."

A very simple solution it was, but it had been vetoed for precisely the reasons she now outlined. "It would be an inconvenience to change my number at this stage. And besides, if that person is intent on harassing me, it would be an easy matter to get the new number as well."

"Have it unlisted—" he persisted doggedly.

"And remain incommunicado? Not a bad thought," she murmured, tongue-in-check, then recalled the delight of the isolation at Max's house in Rockport. But that had been different. There Max had been the only one she'd needed. . . .

Suddenly, the very source of contention rent the air with its shrill jangle. This time Max's hand flew to the receiver before Laura had even released the frying pan.

"Hello!" he barked angrily into the phone, then his furrowed brow, nearly hidden by the haphazard array of brown hair that sleep had mussed, relaxed as the voice identified itself as that of the D.A. A grin of devilry appeared as Max realized he'd been caught with his hands in the cookie jar. "Frank, it's Max Kraig . . ."

Laura gasped. What was Frank going to imagine, with Max here at her apartment on a Sunday morning. Worse, she mused, whatever he could imagine was true! She reached for the phone, only to have Max back out of reach, a solid grip on the mouthpiece.

"What am I doing here?" he repeated Frank's query for Laura's benefit as he sent her a wink. "I'm about to have breakfast for one thing," he began, to a second gasp from the cook, "and, for another, I'm trying to convince this stubborn woman to have her phone number changed." Max had decided to take things into his own hands. "Are you aware . . ."

Laura listened with acute mortification as the tale of her mystery phone calls was retold along with a detailed list of options for what should be done to remedy the situation. At one point Laura, previously rooted to the kitchen floor, hands on jean-clad hips in disgust, reached again for the phone, only to have her embarrassment magnified.

"Excuse me for a minute, Frank," Max began, then barely palmed the mouthpiece as he chided Laura in a loudly seductive tone. "Not now, sweetheart, not now. You will have to be patient." Gallantly he cleared his throat. "Now, where was I . . ."

As it happened, Franklin Potter never did get Laura on the phone. When Max finally hung up, he informed her that the D.A. wanted her in his office early the following morning to discuss the matter. "Said he didn't want to disturb our . . . er, breakfast."

"You're horrible, Max!" she finally exploded in exasperation. "Why did you make those . . . those leading statements . . . all but dangle your motel check-out slip in front of his nose. That was unfair!" Her cheeks, no longer pale, bore the bright blush that Max loved, and he told her so—only adding further to her indignation.

"What did Frank want in the first place?" she finally asked helplessly.

Max grinned sheepishly. "Beats me!"

As morning turned into the afternoon hours, the sheepish grin became a bittersweet memory. The unexpected call from the D.A. had brought reality crashing down upon their heads. Max had said it—"we have a problem here of conflict of interest"—and it was truer than ever. Franklin Potter's call had only brought the matter to a head. Once again Laura wondered why Max had been so blatantly suggestive of their personal relationship to the D.A. It was as though he had been flouting fate, as though he had actually wanted to challenge the situation. Laura's mind whirred back to the first night she had spent in Rockport, when he had likewise been unnecessarily provocative. Had it been callousness or, as she had suspected then, the evidence of a much stronger feeling within him with which he struggled?

As he had stated, Frank was expecting Laura when she arrived at his office first thing the next morning. The very sight of his ruddy cheeks, his formally controlled wisps of thin gray hair high atop his forehead, and his tight, businesslike pose behind his desk signaled the seriousness of his mood.

Beyond the perfunctorally genial greeting which he could never deny her, he made no pretense of pleasantries. "Tell me what's going on between you and Kraig, Laura," he demanded firmly, determinedly. There would be no putting him off this time, she admitted sadly, as her thoughts returned to the heartache of Max's farewell the evening past.

The afternoon had been increasingly tense, each snapping over seemingly petty issues. By the time the evening had arrived and Max packed to leave, Laura was as confused as ever, not about her own feelings, which were unswervingly and pathetically clear, but about those of this enigmatic man for whom she had fallen. As his moods swung from open and caring to cryptic and irritable, so she swung, hanging helplessly at the end of his lifeline.

At the door as she bid him good-bye, he let the punchline fall softly and gently, but nonetheless commandingly. "I think we'd better go our separate ways for a while, Laura." Then in response to the wide blue eyes that involuntarily blinked their distress, he added, "You didn't really think we could go on like this, did you? There is a matter of ethics involved."

Of course he was right. But that made the farewell no easier, the prospect of separation no more bearable. He hadn't kissed her good-bye, but had merely lifted a hand to caress her cheek for a brief, adoring moment before he muttered an oath beneath his breath, turned, and stalked away.

Now, sitting before her good friend and mentor, the pain was as great as it had been at that moment of parting and throughout the night. Emptiness, sadness, loneliness, frustration—it was all back with a vengeance.

"Damn it, I was worried about this!" The D.A.'s vehemence jolted her momentarily out of her torment. What had he seen in her uncurtained gaze of a day-dream? "It's written all over your face, and I know you well enough to recognize it, so don't give me that I-don't-know-what-you're-talking-about look." He paused, eyeing her strangely, obviously uncomfortable with what he felt impelled to ask. "Do you love him?"

The game was up. There was no longer any point in beating around the bush. "Yes." Her tone was soft but filled with certainty.

"Does he love you?"

"I don't know." Her voice was even softer as she looked nervously down at her clenched fists. "Sometimes I think so, other times I'm not as sure." Mustering her courage, she looked up to find Frank in a faraway daze, head turned toward the credenza on which stood the years-old photograph of his wife and children. A melancholy smile tugged at the corners of Laura's lips. "Not quite your usual legal predicament, is it?" The implied apology drew the D.A.'s attention back to her.

"Not quite. But it is a predicament, isn't it?" She nodded disconsolately. "You know," he went on more gently, "that the potential conflict of interest could hurt you, don't you?" Again she nodded. "If you and Max are emotionally tied to one another, there are legitimate grounds to suggest that neither of you will perform up to snuff when that Stallway trial gets going. And although there might never be concrete evidence to that effect, you would have to live with the knowledge, regardless of the verdict on Jonathan Stallway. Can you live with it?"

The silence dragged out interminably as Laura asked herself that question. It had been the one she had doggedly avoided for several weeks now, since she'd acknowledged her love for Max.

Finally, at Frank's gentle prodding, she spoke. "I just don't know. I keep thinking, thinking, but . . . I just . . . don't know." Another silence followed, to be broken by the D.A.'s sigh.

"Look, Laura, why don't you take a day or two off and try to work it out. One way or the other, you've got to make a decision within the week. You can't go on like this—and neither can we. If you remove yourself from the case, we have to give your successor some time to prepare. We could probably get a postponement." These administrative details were all part of the D.A.'s job, yet Laura was several steps behind, lingering dismally on the phrase "if you remove yourself from the case." In the farthest corner of her mind that possibility had bounced around for days; in her heart she had refused to see it. Now, suddenly, she had no choice but to face the possibility that should she decide that her love for the defense attorney would compromise her ability as a prosecutor, she might have to do just that.

"I don't want to take any time off now, Frank," she protested stubbornly, knowing that the time spent brooding would be devastating, that work was her only salvation. And there was plenty of that, totally aside from the Stallway case, to keep her occupied all week. "I will think it over though, and I will have a decision for you in time to prepare someone else, should that be necessary." She couldn't disguise the defeat that weighted her last words. If only she knew Max's feelings, her decision would be so much easier.

"The decision is yours, Laura. I will abide by whatever verdict you reach. I trust your ability to do what is right."

The decision is yours. Of all the times she had

wanted to be in full command of her life, this was not one of them. Yes, the decision was hers, yet she felt at a distinct disadvantage in making it, with the one-sided knowledge she possessed. If she knew Max loved her, the disappointment of withdrawing from her first murder case would be minimal and totally overshadowed by the radiant joy she would feel with the knowledge of his love. If, however, his attraction to her was but a passing fancy, the disappointment would be confounded and, perhaps, unnecessary.

In self-reproachment she caught herself short. This was not the immediate issue, whether or not Max returned her love. The immediate issue was, given her own feelings for him, whether she would be able to function in the legal capacity this case demanded.

"Now"—Frank's authoritative tone recaptured her attention as he reached for his phone— "I want to get Chatfield in here and then you will tell both of us about these phone calls."

Grateful for the temporary reprieve from one quandary, Laura regained her composure by the time Sandy arrived in the D.A.'s office. As commanded, she outlined exactly what had taken place during the two-week period since she had returned from Rockport.

"It's really nothing to worry about," she concluded lightly, only to be pounced upon by both men in quick succession.

"That's a very naive point of view in our line of work, Laura, and you know it," the D.A. scolded, removing his glasses to massage the bridge of his nose.

Sandy supported the contention. "Any number of the guys you've sent to the can in the past three years may be out for a little fun, a little revenge . . . or worse!"

Shuddering at his implication, Laura nonetheless persisted in discounting the possibility. Against her protestations Frank ordered the trooper to research the cases she'd tried, keeping a lookout for any defendants, convicts, or ex-convicts, who may have had a history of this type of harassment. If the calls continued, Frank declared vehemently, they would then have a tap put on her phone.

With that particular problem temporarily taken out of her hands, Laura was free to concentrate on the dilemma which was, in her thoroughly biased view, infinitely more real. After several days of preoccupation and brooding, she began to sense that Frank had known more than she'd given him credit for when he suggested she take some time off; as it was, she did justice to neither her work nor her quandary.

By the end of the week Laura was no closer to a decision. Mercifully, she had retained some control over her powers of concentration, such that her time in court and at the office was fruitful, but her personal state of mind was something else. For not only was she confronted with this all-important decision of whether to face Max in court, but she was also increasingly torn by his absence. Any hope she'd held of his loving her eroded daily. Surely, if he loved her, he would be finding the separation as devastating. Surely he would call. . . .

Saturday came and went, the only calls coming in during her intermittent stops at her apartment, between errands and other chores, being those from a friend and her mysterious follower. The

155

former was a breath of fresh air, the latter a test of patience. Sandy Chatfield's scoring of old files had, as yet, turned up nothing. The calls had remained at the slow-pant stage, however, with no further deterioration into obscenity. For this Laura was grateful. She'd almost grown immune to the sound that had so disgusted her initially, though she realized that in truth she felt some relief knowing that both Frank and Sandy now knew about the calls. And Max . . . Max also knew.

What was she going to do about Max? If only she knew where he was, what he was doing, what his thoughts were it would make her decision so much easier.

How she found herself Sunday morning in the eastbound lane of the Massachusetts Turnpike, she wasn't quite sure. There had been no active decision on her part to drive to Boston; rather, some inner force had directed her. She did not know what she would say to Max if she even found him at home. It was as though she had nothing better to do on this windy March Sunday than to make the two-and-one-half-hour drive to the state capital from Northampton.

Slender fingers gripped the steering wheel to hold the small car steady in the middle lane. Laura forced herself to face the truth, the real reason she sought Max out. She needed his help, as simply as that, in making the decision that faced her. She needed to know, for starters, whether he'd be pleased or displeased to see her. She needed to know what he thought about the prospect of their facing each other in court, though she feared she already had a rough idea on that score. She needed to know whether they

156

could be honest enough with each other to assess their potential for professionalism given the previous intimacy of their relationship.

Helpless, she pondered the mess in which she found herself. Why had she permitted herself to be with Max, to get to know him, finally to fall in love? Given the warning signals at that long-ago arraignment, how could she have succumbed to the temptation he offered? But had it been a matter of will? No, she defended herself staunchly, she'd had no control over her heart. It had been destined, perhaps from that first day in court, that she would fall in love with Max Kraig. And now, still dealing with factors beyond her control, she one by one eliminated the miles between herself and the man who did have control of some of those factors. Once she knew a little more she would make her decision regarding the Stallway case.

Vaguely familiar with the reason-defying traffic pattern of Boston's streets, she carefully wove her way around Arlington, up Boylston, and down Charles streets, to Beacon Hill, from which point a very proper-looking couple directed her to Max's address. Nerve ends quivering in trepidation, she found a parking space, locked her car, and turned to look at the three-story town house in which Max lived and worked. It was typical of those surrounding it, cast of red brick and stone, well kept, dignified though unadorned. The windows were huge, as was the black door that loomed before her—much like its owner.

The wind whipped her hair as she moved up the short walk, bounded on either side by the frozen grass of late winter. She felt cold, then hot, then cold again as she reached out, hesitated, then forced herself to push the small black button just below the brass plate reading MAXWELL KRAIG, ESQ.

She stood for what seemed an eternity, torn between staying and leaving, hoping and despairing, wanting and fearing, before her call was answered. With the sound of a lock being released, the door was drawn back to present to Laura's widened eyes the image of a very tired, very disheveled Max. She must have awoke him. She cringed as she studied his eyes for a reaction to her sudden, unbidden appearance.

At her most optimistic, as she'd weighed the possibilities on the drive east, Max would have burst into his deliciously warming smile and instantly taken her into his arms in ecstatic pleasure. In reality he did not. Rather, an unfathomable expression flitted across his face for a brief moment before being replaced by clear and open anger. Not even in the most pessimistic of those earlier imaginings had she allowed herself to go this far. As the sharp brown eyes impaled her, she felt herself the object of near fury. Unable to function beneath this heart-rending glower, she merely stood and stared frantically up at him.

"What are you doing here?" It was a voice she'd never heard before coming from the lips she knew so well. Its sound was a knife, stabbing her cruelly, its words harsh and grating.

Not knowing quite what to do, she shrugged and made light of his displeasure. "It was an easy drive. There weren't very many cars on the—"

"Why are you here?" he thundered, his force reverberating through her being.

"I had to . . . see you," she murmured haltingly, her breath falling victim to the dagger.

He was pure stone, this man who had once been so warm and soft and giving; now he was cold, dark granite. "Yes?" The jaw was tense and roughened, the lips grim. The slight flaring of his nostrils bespoke his attempts at self-control, at containing the disdain that seeped slowly forth.

Much as she would have liked to, she had come too far to turn and flee. "M-may I come in?" Never had she felt so frightened, yet she invited herself into the lion's den. *It had to be done.* To her chagrin, Max hesitated. Obviously, he did not want to have her in his house. But why? The thought that dawned on her sent a BB ricocheting off the tender walls of her stomach. Quickly, she qualified her request. "I'm sorry, if there's someone—"

"There's no one here," he growled impatiently, though still made no move to step aside and let her in.

With a sigh of defeat her eyes took on a pleading slant. "Please, Max. I won't take much of your time. But I need to talk with you." The desperation of her manner hit its mark. Without a word, his large, solid form stepped to the side in a grudging invitation that she accepted immediately and in spite of its subtle menace. Even as her heart cried out in agony at the certainty that her love was doomed, her mind insisted on the verification of that sentence.

The door closed behind her with a thud, her heartbeat echoing it. She found herself in a square central hallway, closed doors on either side, a longer corridor stretching back, a stairway off it. She turned to see Max standing stiffly by the door in silent indication that the audience would be held here.

"Well?" He wasted no time. The thatch of dark hair that fell across his forehead—the same that in times past had given him a boyish, appealing look—now gave him the air of a tyrant.

She hadn't planned it this way, yet the words tumbled out. "I'm considering removing myself from the Stallway case." She caught sight of the clenched fists at Max's side moments before she felt the pain in her own balled hands and knew it to be the digging of long nails into soft flesh.

"Why would you want to do that?" There finally seemed a drop of annoyance and a perking up of his interest.

How very easy it would have been to say "Because I love you and doubt my ability to function impartially as your opponent." How very easy it would have been, had she wanted to make a complete and utter fool of herself. But the humiliation was too great, even without this final blow, to permit such recklessness. Rather, she became irritated.

"I don't want to do that. I've waited a long time for this case. But I'm not sure I want to face you across the courtroom."

"Why not?" The brown eyes flashed a challenge, not soft and sensual, but hard and daring.

Astonished by his persistence and sudden—and deliberate, she was sure—lack of insight, she stared, open-mouthed at him. "Well, we have been . . . a little more than . . . just friends."

"What difference does that make?"

"What diff—" The words caught in her throat, choking her.

Like the lion readying for the kill, Max straightened and took several steps toward her. Instinctively, she moved back. "What difference does it make that we've been lovers!" he charged callously. "People do it all the time. And for your information, little girl, it has nothing to do with friendship or anything other than a pure and basic physical need." His tone had begun a slow crescendo, anger raising it as he continued. "Are you going to snag your career for that?" The disgust injected in the last word set Laura's stomach to churning. "Are you?" he prodded irately.

Knees trembling now, Laura reached to the bannister behind her for support. "I thought—"

"You thought wrong!" he bellowed, denying her mention of the times—so beautiful they'd seemed then—that they had been together. "And you'll be a damned fool if you let any pitiful romantic notions interfere with the career you're so intent on cultivating." He ran a hand carelessly through his hair in a motion of exasperation. "Go back to Northampton, Laura. I have work to do."

Just as with a life-threatening injury a numbness sets in before the actual pain, so Laura was suddenly protected from the worst of the torment by a shock-cushioning shroud. Immune temporarily from the heartache, she felt a growing will of her own.

"What's come over you, Max? You seem so . . . different." He did look tired and drawn, she noted with well-hid concern.

Avoiding her question, his voice carried a low warning. "You shouldn't have come here."

"Why not?" Now it was her turn; she deserved an explanation.

There was a new element of danger when he met her challenge. "Because I'm not sure I can keep my hands off you. And I'm really not in the

161

mood to play the gentle and considerate lover to your sweet innocence."

Horrified, she gasped aloud. "That's not why I came here! I don't want you to touch me. I just want you to talk to me." With this sudden turn in the conversation, a knot tightened in her stomach.

"Laura, go home. There's nothing to talk about." Max took a step forward to underscore his earlier threat, his face a steel mask. Laura swallowed convulsively as she made a fast decision.

"Thank you. You're right. There isn't anything left to say. You've made it all perfectly clear. And after all, that's why I drove all the way out here." Her words were flowing quickly, her belief in them giving her the strength to go on. "I just want you to know, Max, that I didn't take our relationship as lightly as you did. Had you given the word, I would have gladly given up the Stallway case, given up my whole damned career for that matter." Without mentioning the word *love,* she had all but confessed that deepest, most intimate feeling. Max stood still, several feet before her, a mute statue staring down at her. His anger had dissipated, replaced by a total lack of expression, more puzzling than ever. But Laura was beyond the point of analyzing his mood, so embroiled was she in her own cathartic exercise.

"You know, Max," she went on, tears building behind her lids to diffuse her view, "you may have been right that very first day, when you wondered whether there was truly a private Maxwell Kraig in existence. I thought I'd found one, but I was mistaken. And I can only be grateful that you've helped me discover that error." Laura was totally unaware of the tears now streaming down her cheeks until Max raised a hand to wipe them away. Flinching, she quickly moved away from him and made for the door, her legs lead pipes, her sides jelly.

Entirely swept up into the emotional orbit now, she turned at the door to deliver her final argument. "I'm a good lawyer. I always knew that. And I intend to have Jonathan Stallway put behind bars where he belongs. At least he'll know where he is and why he's there. I doubt you have that advantage. But, then, perhaps I'm partly to blame for that." She looked down briefly, sniffing as she wiped her wet cheeks with both hands. Yes, this would be the hardest part to live with. "You've helped me to become a woman; I only wish I'd been enough woman to help you become the kind of man you could be." Her composure reached its limits; her words died. Simultaneously, Max turned his back on her and walked to the bottom of the stairs, placing one elbow on the bannister, the other hand on his hip, one foot raised on the first step, his head bent over.

Laura could take no more. Leaving the door ajar behind her, she ran along the street to her car, hearing nothing, seeing nothing, aware of nothing but the mechanics of putting the key in the ignition, turning it, revving the motor, and then leaving the home of Maxwell Kraig behind. Far, far behind.

Totally numb, she covered the miles back to Northampton, stopping but once for gas and a cup of hot coffee. She was in a limbo, thinking neither of the past nor the future. The car radio, usually silent, blared its cacophony of news and music, all shallow, all escapist. It was late afternoon when she arrived at her apartment. And there, finally, the reality of what she'd seen, heard, and said hit her.

It began with trembling, to which was soon added nausea, fever, and tears, buckets worth of heartache and heartbreak. She cried into the evening until there were no more tears left. Hunched in bed under piles of blankets, she ignored hunger, cold, and the ringing of the telephone in her bid for oblivion. But comfort was to be a long time coming.

Sleep laid its claim on her misery-racked body intermittently, but by the time morning had arrived and her forehead was as hot as ever, Laura concluded that she was plagued not only by the trauma of a love lost, but by the flu. She dozed, awakening to call the office and inform them of her illness. She even found the strength somehow, to have herself switched through to the D.A.'s office and notify Frank of her decision. She would be trying the Stallway case. Damn it, she would!

The fever had begun to yield to the power of aspirin when late in the morning the phone rang. Knowing that there might be several calls coming in from the office, she weakly struggled out of bed and to the phone.

"Hello?" Her croak sounded horrid, despite her efforts to be the bold, strong Laura her colleagues and friends knew.

"Laura?" Her breath caught at the sound of the deep voice, and she felt a renewed attack of the shakes coming on. "Are you all right? I called the office and they said—"

"I have the flu. I'll be back at my desk tomorrow. Please call me then, if there is some legal matter you have to discuss. Good-bye, Max.'' Bang. Had that been Laura, so cool and businesslike? Had that been Laura, miraculously controlled and unemotional? Had that been Laura, who'd hung up the phone on her only love? Yes! And she would get over him. She would! Why then did she find herself moments later in a pool of tears, when she thought they'd all been long since spent!

Time. It was going to take time, she told herself as she sought comfort, curled up beneath the protection of her blankets. In time she would forget the love she'd known so deeply yet briefly. Forget? No, never forget. Not even get over, for she knew that one part of her would always adore Max. Perhaps learn to live with was the proper phrase. Yes, in time she would learn to live with this everlasting and unrequited love. Maybe even in time she would find an understanding man to fill the overwhelming void this love left. Time, that was all, she reassured herself.

The next morning found her drained of energy, but of normal temperature and impatient intellect. She dressed warmly against the wind and went to the office, determined to let the law do its healing. Back at her desk after several brief court appearances, she was pale, but psychologically revived by the legal exercise. She returned several calls which had come in the day before, and had barely put the receiver down when it buzzed loudly. Absently, she picked it up, her mind still concentrating on an issue the preceding call had raised.

"Yes?" she responded softly, out of habit.

"Laura? You're back at work?" The familiar voice snapped her instantly out of her thought.

Yes, she was back at work and all professional, as Maxwell Kraig had better know.

"It looks that way, doesn't it, counselor," she stated coolly, with a strength which belied her fatigue.

"You're feeling all right?" What an actor the bastard was! She seethed inwardly. This time some of her anger did escape.

"Of course! Why shouldn't I? It was just the flu!"

There was a pause at the other end of the line. "As long as that was all . . ." Sensing some mystery she didn't quite understand, Laura prodded.

"What did you think was wrong? Contrary to your expectation, I didn't fall apart."

His voice was deep, almost hesitant in its gentle chiding. "That wasn't what I expected, Laura. I just wasn't sure whether . . ."

"Whether what?" Had he thought something else unimaginable about her? It wasn't like Max to hedge so, or to give vent to sighs of such obvious resignation as she now heard.

"For a while there I wondered if you might be pregnant." It was spoken almost begrudgingly, this idea that took Laura completely off guard.

"P-pregnant?" she heard herself stammer. The thought hadn't even occurred to her, though she knew for a fact that it was not so. Surprise gave way to indignation, as she realized where his fear lay. "No, Max, I'm not pregnant. You can breathe easily that there will be no embarrassing paternity claim made on you. And even if I were pregnant, I'm not as naive as my previous inexperience may have suggested. There are very simple ways of terminating unwanted pregnancies in this

166

day and age." Appalled by the coldness of her tone and the gist of what she'd said, a wave of weakness attacked her limbs. "No, I'm not pregnant. Was there something else you wanted to ask me?" Her voice reflected the tiredness that dominated her every move now.

"Laura, I—" he began in a softer tone, only to be rudely cut off.

"Legal, Max. Is there anything we need to discuss relating to the Stallway case?"

"No."

"Good-bye, then." It was the second time in as many days that she'd hung up on him, and the satisfaction was as shallow now as before. The big difference was that whereas yesterday had found her at home and able to shed the tears that his call brought on, today she was at the office and had to curb any such show of emotion. Closing her eyes and leaning back in her chair, she took several deep and unsteady breaths, growing more and more distressed as she replayed this latest confrontation.

Surprisingly, the bulk of the distress, in the form of guilt, was directed at herself. For the first time, she'd been driven to say things she hadn't meant. Carrying a child of Max's would never have been an unwanted pregnancy, marriage or no. Nor could she ever have done anything to harm such a child. Of that, she was more sure than anything else of late. No, she certainly was not pregnant, yet she would have rejoiced at the thought of carrying within her Max's seed, of nourishing it to full development, of giving birth and then raising a child whose flesh and blood was part her, part a man who meant so very much to her. In his child she might have had an outlet for the all-abiding love that welled so. As it was, now she felt empty, alone, and bereft of something beautiful.

Eight

Laura passed the week before the trial in a detached haze. Aside from the actual legal preparations, which she attacked with such a vengeance that those assisting her begged for mercy, her life was a rote matter of getting out of the house in the morning and coming home to a makeshift supper and bed at night. Even her Wednesday evening tennis game fell victim to a pair of rubber legs which refused to carry her through a set.

The Saturday routine, albeit unenthusiastically approached, remained the same. There was, however, one bittersweet incident when she picked up her landlady's grocery list and the woman turned to her in curiosity. "Your fella was very worried about you when he called here last weekend." The wizened face livened with expectancy.

"My fellow? Last weekend?"

The old woman put a gnarled finger to her craggy chin. "Now what did he say his name was . . . Crane? You know," she scolded in frustration, "the tall, dark-haired one who carried my bundles that time?"

"Max Kraig? He called here?"

"Yes, missy," Mrs. Daniels answered proudly. "Said he was worried 'bout you, that you'd driven a long way and he wondered whether you'd gotten home in one piece. Said he'd tried your number and there was no answer. That maybe you were sleeping." That would have been when she'd been so out of it, sleeping or not, Laura calculated quickly. "Asked me to look out to see if your car was back, he did," the woman continued, again with the pride of feeling needed. "He felt much better when I told him that the car was in the garage," she concluded with a satisfied smile.

It was little solace that he'd been worried; that was the least he could have been. "Thank you, Mrs. Daniels. I'm sorry he bothered you about it."

"No bother t'all, missy. Glad to help. You tell him to call any time." Laura certainly would *not*, although she gave the woman an appreciative smile for the offer.

In its own way, this incident had been enlightening. For the first time, Laura was able to conjure up Max's image, to hear his name and recall his voice without crumbling. Indeed, as the week progressed, she went through a kind of transformation. As a self-defense mechanism, she became increasingly apathetic to things which had, in the past, aroused her. Originally, the flu bore the brunt of the responsibility for this change, leaving her weakened as it had; as the days passed, however, it became clearly a psychological, rather than a physical, reaction to the emotional trauma through which she'd suffered. Her own personal existence had lost all significance, all importance, all meaning for her. Only law remained.

Law became her outlet—for anger, revenge, bitterness, determination. Into it she poured every ounce of energy. And bolstered by the knowledge that this would be a milestone in her career, she derived much satisfaction from the irony of the situation: It had been her very fear that her feelings for Max would impede her legal performance that had led to the confrontation which was, in large part, responsible for the present zeal which could well make her more effective than ever.

An added complication, a new development in the matter of the anonymous phone calls, occurred on Tuesday night, coincidentally after Frank had agreed to let it ride a bit longer, particularly since the State Police had been unable to come up with any suspect. Laura had come to expect the calls practically every evening. This night was no different. When the phone rang, she neither flinched nor wavered, but lifted the receiver with the emotional lethargy she felt.

"Hello?"

"Your turn's comin', lady." It was a man's voice, low and nondescript. In no way did she recognize it.

"What?" Perhaps she hadn't heard correctly.

"Better start gettin' things in order. It's your turn soon." Click. That was it. Short—too short to trace, even had a mechanism been in operation. Mysterious—neither details nor a possible clue to the caller's identity. Threatening—something else was surely going to follow.

Remaining perfectly calm, Laura phoned the D.A., who received the news of this development from heavy breathing to verbal threats with a good deal more alarm than she could have mustered. Within an hour arrangements had been made to have a tap put on her line. It was obvious that changing the number would only temporarily sidetrack the persistent caller; at least, this way, with him calling regularly, there would be some hope of either tracing the call or recognizing the voice from the recordings that would be made.

Additionally, Frank notified the local police of the situation, ordering that a patrol car keep a close watch on Laura's apartment. Finally, he set the groundwork for a step-up of the detective work which would hopefully reveal the identity of this menace before he revealed himself to Laura. Having been duly informed of these arrangements by her boss in a final call that night, a very cool and unperturbed Laura fell into a deep sleep.

Insulated as she was by her self-induced stupor, she was well rested and thoroughly prepared when she entered the courtroom on Monday morning. Her mind, with its amazing power of selective concentration, had blotted out any apprehension at seeing Max in the flesh once again. He was the defense attorney, she was the prosecutor; it was as simple as that. The repetition of this litany during the last week had successfully imprinted it upon her mind . . . until the actual moment of eye contact threw her a minor setback.

Her attention was on the list of potential jurors when the deep voice intruded, as it had done once before in this very same courtroom.

"Laura?"

It was a deep, velvet melody, as rich as ever. Subconsciously, she had known it would be coming. Slowly and deliberately, she raised her head toward the source of the greeting. In the harsh light of the overhead fluorescents, he looked more lean and tired than when she'd last seen him. His forehead, unbroken by hair, which was obediently parted and neatly combed, carried more worry lines than she'd recalled. He appeared paler. His suit, as always, was dark, distinguished, and immaculate. And, as always, his presence exuded a sense of command, compelling and formidable.

But as before, it was his brown-eyed gaze that held her, glimmering with a warmth she'd imagined gone forever. It was a warmth that threatened to melt the wall of immunity she'd constructed—until she reminded herself that his excitement, like her own, was a product of the drama about to unfold before the judge rather than any personal reaction. The wall remained intact.

"How are you, Max?" she returned coolly.

His dark eyebrows gave the shrug as he cocked his head slightly to the side, then turned his attention to the crowd of people whom the court officers had begun to allow into the courtroom. "Here they come. Are you ready?"

Relieved to be released from his gaze, Laura glanced back over her shoulder at the rapidly filling benches, feeling herself in better humor than she'd been in days, now that she sensed she'd overcome the first, and potentially most hazardous, hurdle of these proceedings. "As ready as I'll ever be," she quipped lightly.

His words were short but sincere. "Good luck." Then he turned and made his way to the defense table, leaving Laura to stare at his back in grudging admiration. He was handsome, her every sense shrieked, before she stifled all reaction and returned to her jury list.

Legally, she held up well. The selection of the jury was completed to her satisfaction by the end of that first day, the opening statements were delivered the following morning. Her father sat in attendance for the latter, bursting with a barely suppressed pride, complementing her afterward on one of the most effective presentations he'd ever heard. Her own praise, however, was unspoken and saved totally for Max, whose words would have had her screaming, had she been a juror, for release of the defendant in a minute, so powerfully chosen and delivered had they been. Even as she feared for the chances of a conviction against such an eloquent opponent, she couldn't help but admire his brilliance.

Actually, this was a pattern that repeated itself many times during the ten days of the trial's duration. Laura conducted herself expertly, presenting a clearcut and concise, though forceful case for conviction. Max, on the other hand, let the burden of proof rest on her, remaining quietly but effectively on the defensive, using the powers of understatement and subtlety to cast reasonable doubt on her arguments.

As the days passed, Laura put forward her case, Max cross-examined her witnesses; she recalled one or two, and finally rested. Then it was Max's turn to rebut the case she had skillfully built. There were character witnesses testifying to the good name and deeds of Jonathan Stallway, and scientific witnesses, casting doubt on the cause and nature of the scuffle that had allegedly led to the girl's death. When finally the defense rested, Laura knew that her final argument would be crucial to her ultimate success.

It was at the midway point in the trial, as Max

began to present his case, that Laura realized herself to be more vulnerable to his presence, personally, than she'd hoped. For increasingly during the non-court hours, her thoughts centered on him—how talented a lawyer he was, how positively handsome he looked, how warm and giving he had the potential to be, how exquisite a lover he'd proven himself. Yes, as much as she hated to admit it, she found the physical frustration as trying as the emotional. To see him each day and not touch, hold, love . . . it was a torment which steadily increased. Sleep came harder despite her exhaustion after a full day's proceedings, and by the end of the first week, makeup had become a necessity for concealing the dark hollows beneath her eyes and brightening her pale, drawn look.

To her dismay, Max thrived under the same pressure which so devastated Laura. He seemed more and more rested as each day passed, his own coloring had improved, and he appeared to relax as the trial progressed. He was in his element when he presented his case to the jury, when Laura had no choice but to watch his tall, good-looking form as it strode confidently from the defense table to the witness stand, the judge's bench, or the jury box, or to hear his sonorous tone as its timbre varied appropriately and effectively before each audience. He could be humble before the judge, confidence-inspiring before the jury, as gentle and coaxing before his own witnesses as he was pointed and commanding before those of the prosecution.

The anger and bitterness that had driven her earlier, had faded into oblivion by the time the final arguments were given. Rather, dedication to the law had taken over to spark her own final statement with a persuasive power that held its own magnificently, coming as it had on the heels of Max's eloquence.

That final argument was her moment of glory. Not only was it instrumental in congealing the facts of the case in the jurors' minds such that, after eight hours of deliberation, they returned a verdict of guilty to a charge of manslaughter, but it was also the most confident moment she would have for a while.

To Laura, there was victory neither in the verdict nor in the conclusion of this trial, which had so profoundly affected her life. The verdict had actually been satisfactory for *both* the prosecution and the defense; the defendant had been found guilty and would spend time in prison, though his sentence, by virtue of the lesser charge, was not to be as harsh as it might otherwise have been.

Clearly, she was torn. With modesty and grace she accepted the kudos of her colleagues. Inside, however, she ached at the knowledge that the trial's end would subject her, cold turkey, to the withdrawal of Max's presence in Northampton. As much as the sight of him each day had pained her increasingly, there had been that heart-stopping anticipation each morning, the same stomach-jumping and knee-weakening that his appearance always had on her—a lovely feeling she couldn't deny. Now it would be no more. Deep inside, she died just a little bit.

Her small office was a dismal place late that afternoon. The celebration had ended, the celebrants had left, the newspapers had been fed their ration of detail, the phone had finally quieted.

All that remained was for her to go home to a much deserved rest . . . and her own prison of loneliness and despair.

In a last-ditch effort to postpone the inevitable, she headed upstairs to her favorite spot of peace and solitude, the library. Now she had no work to do; she hadn't even brought her briefcase with her. Rather, she sat down and replayed the soul-reaching happenings of the past three months. No longer was she protected by the numbness that had cushioned her earlier; she was on her own now and very vulnerable.

The stark emptiness of her future loomed as a terrifying reality. How deeply she had loved, how deeply she loved still, as much as she tried to fight it. How could she cope with the knowledge that Max would vanish from her life for good?

She loved and needed Max, yet he neither loved nor needed her. That particular reality had been made painfully clear to her that fateful Sunday afternoon in Boston. Wanting was something else. Each wanted the other physically; it was a chemical reaction that would always exist. Yet that alone Laura could not abide. It had to be all or nothing where her battered heart was concerned.

Restless, she stood and walked to the window, sliding down onto its broad sill. The second-floor vantage point gave her a clear view of the main street, bathed now in the gleaming film of a gently falling April shower. Perhaps she should go to Chicago, to be with her father for a while. Perhaps a week or two away from these all-too-raw memories would be enough. . . .

"Laura?"

With a start, she twisted her head toward the

door. It was a moment of déjà vu; she had been startled in this room once before. Max had remembered, too, her objections on that other day. This time he stood in the doorway, a full room's length from her.

The velvet peal of his voice, coming as it had fresh upon those thoughts of pain and heartbreak, brought a well of tears to her crystal blue eyes. Turning her head back to the window, she struggled to contain them.

"I'd like to talk to you. May I come in?"

A shrug was the only response she was able to make. In turn, his blurred form approached, his long limbs relaxing against the edge of the table nearest her, the sound of his voice suddenly too close for comfort.

"I believe congratulations are in order," he began softly. "You were fantastic in there. Your case was solid and well presented. Your final argument was one of the most persuasive I've heard. The conviction was well-deserved."

A resurgence of the old bitterness held her tears in check enough to finally allow her to speak. "Don't patronize me, Max. You know as well as I do that against any other defense attorney, it would have been a second-degree, if not a first-degree, conviction. You are the one who deserves the congratulations." With misted eyes glued to the street below, she was surprised by her own hostility. Determinedly, she avoided his gaze, in part out of fear of what it could do to her, in part out of fear of his seeing her own weakness.

"Then we share the victory." The sound of his voice had neared, the vibrations from his body placed him no more than an arm's length from her. He spoke in the low croon that sent a shiver from head to toe of her sensitive body. "Don't you see, baby, we did it!"

Rage flowed through Laura with breakneck speed. Oblivious to the lingering tears that lined her lids, she turned to glare at eyes whose softness instantly froze. For the first time, she sensed her own power, and she set out determined to use it. "I am not your baby," she seethed through gritted teeth, "and we did nothing more than any other two lawyers would have done. In addition, there's something totally immoral to talk of victory, when an innocent young girl has been murdered, a pathetic young man has been sent to a prison where he will no doubt come to wish he had been the victim."

Startled by her anger, Max took a step back, jamming his fists into his pockets. "You misunderstand me, Laura," he went on to explain slowly. "We made it through the trial in top form, you and I. We were both able and effective . . . despite our . . . personal relationship."

Laura cringed visibly at his reminder. "There is no personal relationship, Max. You saw to that." Again, the extent of her bitterness came to the fore.

"Laura, about that day—"

"Don't say anything! Please! I don't want to hear." Tensing her jaw determinedly, she turned her head away from him back to the window. The lights of early evening had begun to appear, spattering long and brightly colored streaks across the wet pavement below. On these Laura centered her concentration, unaware that the image had been made all the more impressionistic by her own tear-filled gaze.

When steel-boned fingers took her chin to turn

her face back to his, she resisted momentarily, then faced him rebelliously. His expression mirrored her own pain, though she was too absorbed to see it. In a gesture of disdain, she jerked her chin up enough to be freed of his grasp, and after a stunned moment, his hand fell limply to his side.

"I never thought I'd see such bitterness in you. Do you . . . resent me as much as that?" His jaw clenched convulsively as he awaited her answer.

"Resentment is one word. There are others which could fit," she snapped.

His tone melted into sadness, forcing a new shaft of pain into Laura's heart. "Do you know what fascinated me most when I first met you? That unique blend of strength and softness held together by a spirit I'd never seen before in a woman." She held her breath, steeling herself against his gentle persuasion. "What's happened to the spirit, Laura? This new one is negative, very different from the positive one I so admired. And the softness? Has it gone for good?"

His breath fanned her face, he had moved so close. As much as Laura fought its pull, his magnetism—the same one that had so captured her when she'd first met him—was a potent force, threatening to subject her to one final humiliation.

With the few lingering shards of resistance, she confronted him, outward calm her greatest challenge. "It's no good, Max—that tone, those words. I've seen you in action now, in the courtroom and out, and I know how well you perform. You charmed the judge, the jury, and the witnesses right from under my nose. I won't let you manipulate me again. It's over, Max. Leave it." They were the last words she wanted to say or hear, yet she could not bear his sugar-coating any longer, knowing as she did his true feelings toward her. Her knees had begun to tremble despite the conviction she felt. Worse, the tears that had momentarily receded now reappeared, filling her tormented blue eyes to the brink.

The anguish in his own eyes was clear, yet its cause was a mystery Laura had not the strength to probe. She felt weak, tired, distraught. Her brief show of resistance had thoroughly drained her. There was only pain left.

His voice was an agonized whisper. "I'm sorry, Laura, if I've done this to you." She put her head down to blot out his form, though his words tore into her. "I never meant to hurt you. You have to believe that. I'm sorry, baby." That was her undoing, the endearment that represented everything she'd had, then lost.

Slowly, head still bowed tightly, tears began to fall. Silent sobs erupted to rack her trembling body. With a soft cry of misery, she covered her face with her hands. It was the same torment, loving him and hating him, wishing he'd go away and wishing he'd take her in his arms. How was she ever to survive this heart-rending tug-of-war?

The matter was taken out of her hands at that instant, as Max took her into his arms, cushioning her tear-soaked face against the skin-warmed softness of his shirt. One large hand covered the back of her head, holding her firmly against his chest, the other gently massaged her shoulders and back in a gesture of comfort. He was silent, letting the support of his body and the inherent soothing of his nearness do whatever superficial healing was possible.

She had no idea how long she cried, only grateful for the quiet comfort that Max offered. When her tears subsided, she clung to him for a moment longer, grasping at a closeness that would soon be but another memory never to be relived. It was with a final, spasmodic sniffle that she stepped back and accepted the clean, white handkerchief he offered, clinging to it, in turn, long after her eyes and cheeks had been dabbed dry.

Slowly, Max paced the floor to the door and back, his movement reflecting his own indecision. When finally he came to a standstill in front of her, he made no effort to touch her. "Let's go get your coat. I'm taking you home."

Reflex forced Laura back a step. "No!"

"Look, Laura—" he began, placing both hands on her shoulders.

"Don't touch me!" she begged, squirming from his grasp as the horror of his implication hit her. Did he really think she was that weak that she'd tumble back into bed with him—after all he'd said that day in Boston? "Don't touch me," she repeated in a hysterical whisper, her hands frantically clasping the windowsill behind her.

Recognizing her potentially explosive state, he backed off, walking halfway across the room before turning to face her, hands thrust into his pockets. "I'm not going to touch you, Laura," he sighed. "I merely want to see you safely home. You're tired and upset. I know you don't drive to work, and it's pouring, in case you hadn't noticed. I could call Chatfield to drive you, but frankly, I don't trust him to see that you get something to eat, a hot bath, and a good night's sleep."

"Why should I trust you?" Tired and upset

she might well be, but she hadn't yet lost her ability to reason.

The brown-eyed gaze was long and hard, searching into her very depths with painful intensity. "Because, deep down inside, you know how I feel." She did. She knew that he found her to be interesting and able . . . but that was all. She also knew, deep down inside, that he wouldn't physically harm her. What frightened her was the extent of her own weakness. Could she hold out against him, there in the intimacy of her own apartment?

Closing her eyes in weariness, she shook her head sadly. "No, Max. I can get home alone. I want to be alone."

"I understand, Laura. But I'd feel better—"

"I don't care what you'd feel." She hadn't dreamed she had the strength to spark again, yet somehow Max had a knack of pushing her to extremes. Now there was a warning in her blue eyes. "I'm mainly concerned with what I feel right now, and I have every intention of walking home by myself, rain and all. I need the fresh air." Fearful of losing her stamina before she could make good her vow, she made a hasty exit from the library.

Naturally adverse to elevators on the theory that every added bit of exercise would do her good, she ran down the two flights of stairs to her office, swung on her trenchcoat, retrieved her briefcase and umbrella, and made her escape. To her relief, there was no sign of Max.

The walk to her apartment was not long, and the unseasonally cool air was refreshing at first. But she had underestimated the strength and steadiness of the rain, and by the time she reached her own street, she was chilled to the bone and soaked despite her umbrella.

It was inevitable that this physical discomfort should affect her temper, unpredictable of late under even the best of conditions. With each passing step, she became more and more cross at none other than her heart's obsession, the man whom she had just stalked so determinedly away from. *What gall the man had,* she had glowered under the privacy of her umbrella. He would have gladly driven her home and bedded her, for the mere physical satisfaction of the act. He himself had once suggested that his life was shallow, and she'd refused to believe it. No more!

And who was he, she demanded silently, stomping inadvertently into a huge puddle cloaked by the darkness, then swearing hoarsely as the muddy water reached her hem in haphazard spatters—who was he to accuse her of being hard and bitter? Hadn't he been the cause of her transformation? Hadn't he shown her how the true bastard operated?

The wind had begun to pick up as she covered the last of the distance. Lowering her head against it, she kept her eyes to the pavement. It was a momentary shock, therefore, when a pair of rain-dotted loafers entered her field of vision, rooted, no less, to the welcome mat outside her own front door. If it wasn't the master of hypocrisy himself, she rued cynically!

"Let me have your keys, Laura." The command was firm, overriding her annoyance at literally running into him on her doorstep. Teeth chattering, fingers stiff from the cold, she pointed to the large pocket of her coat. Comprehending the simple sign language, he reached in, withdrew the round brass key ring, and unlocked the door. Her stiffened hands never felt him take the umbrella she'd been clutching so fiercely. Without a word she allowed herself to be escorted up the stairs and into her living room where, while she peeled off the drenched raincoat, Max saw to the lights and the heat.

"Crazy New England weather," he muttered under his breath as he peeled off his own coat, took Laura's from her dripping fingers, and draped both over the backs of chairs to dry.

"What are you doing here?" she demanded irritably, unconsciously kneading her hands to revive their circulation. She had already stepped out of her thoroughly soaked pumps, and now stood in stockinged feet looking the distance up at her nemesis. His expression was unfathomable, his features set, his eyes a depth of murky brown.

"I told you that I was going to see you safely home, and that is exactly what I've done."

"Were you following me?"

"Round and about."

"Damn it, I was cold and wet. Why didn't you pick me up when you saw how hard it was raining? Is that how you see someone safely home? I could catch pneumonia, and there you were in your warm, dry Mercedes. That's what I call true gallantry!" Her anger, ludicrous as it was in light of her blunt rejection of his offer earlier, was an extension of the strain she'd been under, in general, and the rigor of the walk home, in partic-ular. Now she stormed toward her bedroom to remove her wet clothes—only to stop short after several steps and turn on him in renewed ire. "And now that you've seen me *safely home*"— she exaggerated the words as she stood with her

184

hands on her hips—"you can just get your coat back on and leave."

With maddening perseverance he slowly shook his dark head, small beads of moisture glistening on his hair. "I also told you that I was going to see that you have a hot bath, something to eat, and a good night's sleep, in that order."

Suddenly struck by a wave of fatigue, she breathed a long sigh. "I'm so tired, Max. Just go home and let me be."

To her chagrin, he proceeded to remove his suit jacket and toss it on a chair by his coat before heading for the kitchen. "The bath!" he ordered over his shoulder, leaving her in a state of utter frustration. She really was exhausted. But, she reasoned, perhaps he would finally leave her to her private misery if she complied with his demands.

Taking care to lock the bathroom door, a precaution she'd never had to take before in her own apartment, she slid into a hot tub generously laced with fragrant bath oil. If relaxation was possible, she vowed, she'd make the most of this obligatory soak! What she hadn't planned on was falling asleep, neck deep in water and suds, head cradled on the curved lip of the tub. It was only a heavy pounding on the bathroom door that saved her from water log, or worse.

"Laura! Have you fallen asleep?" he called in mocking accusation.

"Of course not," she lied groggily.

"Then get out here while dinner is still hot!"

The brief moments of sleep—of complete and utter relaxation—had mellowed her mood. She still knew Max to be the enemy, but she was now a more compliant prisoner. Her mind was very nearly a blank as she dressed in her long—prim he had called it once—flannel nightgown and equally as concealing bathrobe. It was only as she opened the bathroom door that it occurred to her that there was little food in the house to begin with. What was it that smelled so good?

"It's just as well you, ah, fell asleep. The delivery man was delayed in this rain. I ordered yours with pepperoni and onion. If that's not right, you can have my sausage, pepper, onion, and double cheese." He grinned in a rare gift of ear-to-ear whiteness. In astonishment, she looked past him to her pizza-laden table, as he went on. "At least you had some wine in the house. No food. Just drink. That's terrific for the health, you know!" he scolded gently.

Salivating at the scent of the tempting fare, she silently walked to the table, and tucking one leg beneath her, sat down before the pepperoni and onion. "Are you sure you've got enough goo on yours?" she asked tartly, extending her wineglass toward the proffered bottle.

"I'm not sure. But I haven't eaten as appetizing a meal in days. And from the looks of your refrigerator, neither have you." Laura merely shrugged as she attacked her pizza, suddenly acutely hungry. He was right; she hadn't eaten as delicious a meal in too long, though it was only fair to give some credit to the hot bath, which had so relaxed her, and the wine, which carried on that chore.

"How are your tennis kids doing?" he deftly sandwiched conversation and pizza.

"As saucy as ever." She avoided his gaze as she focussed on her own meal. "They ask for you all the time."

186

A slow smile twisted the corner of his mouth. "Oh? You must just love that!"

"Uh-huh! I tell them you broke a leg falling out of bed," she dead-panned. "They think that's hysterical."

"I bet! Not too good for the image, though, is it?"

"I doubt there's any need for worry. These kids never squeal to the media." Her sarcasm brought a tightening to his jaw, though he let the barb pass. His thoughts were on to other things, and his subsequently sober expression reflected them.

"Laura, what do you want in life?" The abrupt change of subject brought her head up sharply. When she made no move to answer, he reworked his question. "If you could plan out the next five, ten years of your life, what would you most want to do?"

There was no further hesitation. "Get married. Have a family." The thoughts were her own, yet Laura was as startled by them as Max.

"You're kidding."

"No." Strangely, she wasn't.

"What about your career, it means so much to you." He was puzzled, his brown-eyed gaze scrutinizing her.

"It did."

"Did?" Dark brows arched dubiously.

Laura's eyes dropped to watch her slender fingers slowly trace the tines of a fork. "It's still important, but, I guess, it has to be put in perspective."

"And?" His velvet-soft voice coaxed her on.

With a spurt of defiance, she looked straight

187

at him. "And I'd like to have a husband—and lots and lots of children."

"Lots and lots?"

"Yes."

"Wouldn't one or two do?"

"At one time, yes. All told, no."

"Why not?"

How strange, she mused, that she should be learning so much about herself in this way. It was as though she were a split image, one watching and hearing, the other talking. With interest she awaited her next explanation. It flowed as spontaneously.

"I want a large family—many faces and much love. I'd like to have warmth and happiness. Perhaps there is security in numbers. I don't want myself or any of my family to ever face the loneliness, the emptiness . . ." Appalled by what she was about to confess, she let her low whisper trail off, dropping her eyes to avoid his visual probe. She was voluminously clothed, yet naked before this man, very alone and utterly vulnerable.

The silence was deep. Neither of them moved, each immersed in thought. It was Max who finally spoke, his voice carrying a poignancy unusual for him.

"I had no idea you felt that way."

Laura laughed sadly. "Neither did I. It's strange; you spend years of your life working toward one goal and then, when you finally reach it, you find that it's only a small part of something much bigger." She'd been talking as much to herself as to him. Embarrassed, she lifted her head with a small shake, and threw the ball back at him. "What about you? Does law give you that

188

sense of fulfillment? You've been a lawyer much longer than I have.''

Rocking his chair back onto its two rear legs, Max put his hands in his pockets and smiled. "Wait a minute now. I'm not quite over the hill.''

Unable to resist his smile, she answered it with a surprisingly soft one of her own. "You know what I mean. Are you pleased with your life? What do you hope to be doing in five or ten years?''

"That's a very good question.'' Was that humor dancing in his eyes?

"And the answer?''

"I'm working on it.'' Definite humor there was, with an added twinkle for good measure.

Exasperated, Laura raised both hands. "Is that all you have to say? I've painted my life out before your eyes in vivid colors, and you can't even begin to make a pencil sketch of yours?'' She was oddly annoyed.

"Does it matter to you?''

"Yes. No. I mean, if nothing else, I'd like to know what makes such an illustrious personality tick!'' Her irritation was instantly matched by hardened features and an angry retort.

"I'm no illustrious personality!'' The front legs of his chair hit the floor with a bang, though Laura was beyond intimidation.

"Then what are you, Max? What do you want out of life?''

He glared at her. "I want many of the same things you do, Laura. I'm human!''

Emboldened by the knowledge that this man would be conclusively leaving her life within the next few hours, she stood up staunchly and put both hands before her on the table. "Are you?

I'd never know it! You seem immune to the things that matter to most of us mortals, such as love and pain, joy and loneliness. You can switch things on and off at will—warmth, compassion, involvement." She paused, straightening, and narrowed her blue gaze. "You know, I think you're afraid. You're afraid to commit yourself to anybody or anything on a truly personal level. I think that's why you can pour so much energy into causes like . . . like the Wilkins Home—you can feel vicariously all of the sentiments we simple folk feel, then when the going gets too tough, you can withdraw behind the public image. Is that it, Max? Are you satisfied to live life through the pain and suffering and, yes, joy of others?"

"No, damn it!" The force of his seething reply took her off guard, though later she was to wonder whether she'd expected to escape retaliation for her outburst. Now she watched with rounded blue eyes as he stood, pulled himself up to his towering height, then began to move around the table toward her. "No, I have every intention of living life myself." Instinctively, Laura recognized the smoldering glimmer in his eyes, the suggestive undertone of his deep words. She moved back and began to shake her head.

"No, Max. No. Don't come near me. Please . . . don't." Her plea went unheeded as he stepped within inches of her tensed form. Terrified by some animal instinct, she swung around to flee this glowering mask of impassioned rage, only to find her arm snagged in his iron fingers, long, strong, and digging into her soft flesh. "Don't! Let me go, Max?" He said nothing, the rigid set of his mouth telling the story.

Pulling her along behind him, he headed for

her bedroom, deaf to her desperate cries of protest. She tried to pull away from his grasp, but he only tightened it until she thought her bones would snap.

Hard hands swung her around, then threw her upon the bed. On the rebound she tried to rise, only to be crushed by the weight of his dark and menacing body. "Max, please," she begged a final time, "don't do this—" Her breath was cut off by his mouth, clamping down with angry force, punishing her lips for some unknown crime.

Laura's mind and body were firm allies. Her thoughts were filled with revulsion, shame, and degradation. Her body fought him unrelentingly, squirming beneath him, battering him with her arms. When he finally lifted his mouth from hers, she gasped, panting in terror as much as from lack of oxygen.

Max's own breathing was ragged, yet his anger filtered clearly through his glower. "Oh, I'm very human, Laura, and I intend to feel and do everything in life."

Her mouth had opened in renewed plea when his plundered it again. This time his hands began a rough and aggressive assault on her body, causing her pain at every touch. She would never know where she found the continued strength to fight him; all her energies seemed wasted against his immovable granite form. She was no match for his physical superiority. Yet something within would not let her surrender, not as long as she remembered how very beautiful it had all been once, a dream ago.

His hard body was atop hers now, his muscled thighs parting her own even as his hands lowered to violently lift up the hems of her robe and night-gown, forcing them above her hips, before reaching for the fastening of his trousers. Panic hit her as the air touched her bare skin. Yet her struggles had taken their toll, her strength had been spent, she had nothing left with which to fight. Nothing at all . . . except her own agonizingly soulful plea, uttered in a strangled tongue.

"I love you, Max. Please don't do this to me. Just let me keep the memories . . . please . . . I love you."

Even before she'd finished, she felt his body stiffen, then roll away to sit up on the far edge of the bed, head hung low, breath coming in shuddering gasps. Awash with humiliation both at what he'd nearly done and what she'd clearly said, Laura struggled to the other side of the bed and jumped up, staggering to the bathroom in time to be violently ill. It was a nightmare that would never end, she moaned silently, as she braced herself for oncoming spasms.

Much later, when the retching had finally ceased and she'd splashed her face with cold water for the third time, she ventured to open the bathroom door and step out, intent only on bringing the doomed relationship to its sorrowful and inescapable end as quickly as possible. She loved Max Kraig with her very heart and soul, yet there was no way she could reconcile that love with the anger and disdain he'd shown he felt for her.

As at so many other times during their ill-fated affair, however, Max had already taken things into his own hands. He was gone. There was sign of him neither in the bedroom, nor the kitchen, nor the living room. He'd taken his jacket and his trenchcoat. The only lingering evidence of his presence on this dismal night were the cold remains of a half-eaten pizza . . . and the raw and open sores of an aching heart.

Nine

In actuality it was a sizeable legacy he left her. It was a legacy of beautiful memories, of love and passion, of desire and ecstasy, of nearness and the myriad means of communication two lovers could find. It was a legacy of experience, both private and public, personal and professional, encompassing all she'd learned from their brief liaison. It was a legacy of pain, of hurt and heart-ache, of humiliation and distrust, of frustration and disillusionment, of the sheer hell of a loneliness made worse by comparison with what might have been. And, finally, there was the small gold heart she wore constantly, ruby-eyed and shining, a poignant reminder of that part of her own heart which was, now and forever, lost.

For days he was her life's obsession. Her emotions teetered from love to hate, from anger to fear. She felt confused and out of control, a state which, in itself, was painful. Her personal life was in shambles; her professional life suffered the fallout.

"Snap out of it, Laura!" Her trooper-in-atten-dance finally brought the issue to the surface a week later. "You've been a walking zombie since the trial. We've got three other cases here"—he tapped the thick folders on her desk which dealt with the cases they were to be discussing at the moment—"that badly need your attention . . . your full attention."

Laura's features were suddenly open and vulnerable, in noted contrast to the austere pull of her dark black hair into its somber bun. Sandy's perceptiveness was keen, and she knew him to be right. Clearly, he spoke as a friend.

"It's Kraig, isn't it?" The harshness in his tone served to soften her own. After all, Max wasn't here to defend himself. Instinctively, her hand went to the small gold heart that lay against the creamy smoothness of her throat.

"Oh, it's not all that bad." Despite its sadness, the gentleness of her words surprised her.

Sandy eyed her warily. "I knew the guy was dangerous."

"He's not dangerous, he's simply . . ." How futile it would be to try to describe Maxwell Kraig in a word, even two; nothing about the man was simple.

"Simply what?"

"Oh, nothing."

"You know," he began, his expression calculating as he fitted in the pieces of a long-strung-out jigsaw, "there's been a change in you since you met him. You're more sensitive . . . more feminine, I guess, is the right word."

A wan smile answered his gaze. "I'm not sure whether to take that as a complement or an insult."

"Just an observation, kid."

"Not along the usual line, though, is it?" Her casual quips were designed to avoid the central issue; Sandy would have no part of it.

"I'm speaking as a man, Laura, not a detective.

I only wish those faraway looks were for me. They're soft and sad and . . . beautiful." His own eyes held a caring Laura had never seen in them before. She was touched but also acutely aware of the deeper implication.

"Sandy—"

He held up a hand in silent protest. "I know, I know. We're just friends. But I hope that someday I'll find a woman to look at me the way you look at him." She flinched visibly, but he seemed not to notice. "Are you still seeing him?"

This time, the flinch was awesomely internal, sending a shaft of pain through her. "No."

The other hesitated a minute, wrestling with his own impulses before yielding to them. "Look, I know this is none of my business, but . . . why? The vibes between the two of you were pretty strong there for a while, and it's obvious you still—"

"No." The melancholy sound that cut him off, soft as it was, had its effect.

"Your decision or his?" He took a different tack, his feelings for Laura, ones of warmth and an urge to protect, driving him on.

"It was a mutual decision." Her blue-eyed gaze had shifted from the trooper to some faraway place, such that she missed the skeptical eyebrow that shot up.

"Mutual? Then why the trouble concentrating on your work? Having second thoughts?" The softness of his tone eased the directness of his inquiry.

"No!"

Again Sandy's gaze was searching. "It hurts, doesn't it?"

Suddenly, the conversation hit too close to

home. An impatient sigh cut through her lips. "Sandy, I think it's best left alone. I really don't want to talk about it."

"That bastard . . ." he muttered. "They're a slimy bunch, those arrogant, high-priced ones."

Again, she felt an inexplicable need to defend Max. "That's unfair, Sandy. He's a moral person—"

"He's a bastard in my book!"

Laura shrugged. There was no way she would change Sandy's mind. He had been distrustful from the start; his instincts had proven more accurate than hers. Perhaps he was right too. Max had been a bastard in many ways!

"Ah-hah! See, you agree with me!" There was triumph in the trooper's grim exclamation. Laura couldn't help but smile.

"You're almost as bad as he is! Men!" she snorted gently, opening the first folder on her desk and flipping over the top papers.

"There's one more thing, Laura, before we get going on those. You haven't even asked about the progress on identifying your mystery caller."

Impatiently, she defended herself. "I really haven't thought that much about it."

He stared at her incredulously. "How can you not think about it, when you get threatening phone calls every night?"

"It's let up a bit. He doesn't call every night any longer—now it's only three or four times a week. I think he's getting bored with the whole game, just as I am."

The trooper growled begrudgingly, "Three or four times a week is plenty. And he may not be bored, just sly. We've gotten nowhere tracing the call. The guy is pretty wise; he hangs up just before we can get a track on him.''

Sensing that her friend blamed himself for the lack of leads, Laura put a hand out to cover his. ''Look, Sandy, it's nothing you or any of the others can help. And I'm not bothered by the calls. Really!''

In all honesty she wasn't. The calls, ominous and intimidating as they were objectively, fulfilled some strange need to flirt with danger that Laura felt. Falling short of self-destructive, her apathy toward the potential hazard was, given her internal upheaval, not unusual. Only later would she look back on her attitude as irresponsible; only later would she understand that she must have wanted something, anything to happen, to prove to herself that some part of her was still alive. As for the rest of life, she avoided it whenever possible, withdrawing into her own torture-ridden shell.

Later in the following week, nearly two weeks after the conclusion of the trial, Franklin Potter called her into his office. ''What's this about Timothy Reardon handling the sentencing of the Stallway case for you?'' he demanded, tapping a finger on the revised list of case assignments. ''Any special reason?''

She shrugged. ''He sat in on so much of the trial; I thought he'd enjoy handling it.''

As a politician, the D.A. could worm his way around most issues if he wished. He could also, however, recognize when someone else did it. ''Laura, I wondered why you didn't want to handle it,'' he scolded over the brim of his glasses.

''No special reason,'' she lied with too-nonchalant a flip of the head.

197

Adept in his own right in the art of cross-examination, Frank cleared his throat. "Let me reword that. Are you and Max Kraig . . . still . . . ?" Her blue eyes came up with a start, pain searing in them long enough for her boss to see it before she averted them. "I see. It ended badly, did it?" He knew her too well, this old family friend, for Laura to be anything but truthful.

"You might say that." Defeat was written over her ivory-sculpted features.

"I'm surprised. I really thought this was it."

"So did I. For a while . . ." Both her eyes and her hands remained cemented to her lap.

"What happened?" It could have been her own father asking the question, so full of gentleness and concern was his tone.

"I don't know," she began, only to correct herself immediately. "Yes, I do. It's very simple. I fell in love; Max did not."

"Are you so sure?"

"Oh, yes, very sure."

"How can you tell?"

Blushing, she knew she could not explain adequately. The pain and humiliation were still too fresh. "Oh, things he said. And did." She evaded the details. "He's just not the type to settle down, I guess."

The D.A. looked genuinely puzzled. "That's strange. I thought he'd finally found . . ." His voice trailed off as he realized he'd said too much.

"Frank, you were the one who warned me about him in the beginning! And you were absolutely right! How can you be doubtful now?"

He sat forward in his chair. "He's called me several times . . . about you."

Her heart froze. "About me?"

"He was—is—worried."

"Is?"

The D.A. nodded. "I heard from him just yesterday. He's been in and out of the state and wanted to make sure everything was all right here."

Laura's heart had begun to thud loudly. "All right?"

"You know, the phone calls and all."

"Oh." What had she expected? He was merely curious! And he and Frank were friends to start with. How perfectly normal that he should call.

"Still," Frank went on, confusing her all the more, just when she thought she'd figured this one out, "from the way he talked, I could have sworn he was as taken with you as . . ." As before, he abruptly severed his rambling.

"He's a great actor, isn't he!" she barked, angry anew. Bolting out of her chair, she paced to the window, arms folded protectively across her chest, one hand clutching at the small gold heart round her neck. After several moments of deafening silence, she spoke, more softly, her anger replaced by a defeat-laden conviction. It was the swing of the pendulum that threatened to maim her; she could not take the wavering from hope to despair a moment longer. "I don't want to see him, Frank. That's why I've asked Tim to cover for me. I don't want to see Max again!"

As the next days passed, it appeared she was to have her wish. She neither saw him, heard from him, nor read about him in the newspapers. Not that her thoughts ever strayed far from him, but it was her only hope that, in time, that too would change.

The day of the Stallway sentencing came and

went. Laura stayed as far from the office as possible that day, setting up a slew of appointments outside Northampton. After all, she had reasoned, the sentencing was a relatively simple matter. She had prepped her stand-in on her own recommendations, and was pleased to discover, when she called in to the office late that afternoon, that the judge had acceded to the prosecution's request. She was also surprised—and the slightest bit disconcerted—to learn that Max had avoided the hearing too, sending one of his associates, with no excuses given. But, that was no longer her business, she reminded herself sharply, even as part of her wondered where he was and why he hadn't made a final show. Her only conclusion was that he had no further desire to see her, either. And this thought, this vivid reminder of his underlying disdain for her, gnawed at her.

The first of May brought with it warm air, pale green buds, and brightly colored blossoms. The world was gay and fresh, the dismal chill of winter having yielded to the exquisite wonder of spring.

Not so for Laura. Spring was bypassing her this year, that gray chill remaining within her, packed firmly and immovably around her heart. She went through the motions of replacing the woolens in her closet with cottons and linens, of storing her snow tires for another six months, of turning off the radiators and lowering the screens. Yet there was nothing but winter at her very core.

Friends began to express their concern more frequently. Was she feeling well? She looked too pale. Was she working herself too hard? She looked too tired. Was she eating at all? She looked too thin. As for herself, she avoided the mirror whenever possible, knowing that the observations were correct, yet unable to remedy the situation. She seemed incapable of corraling her resources, of pulling herself out of her depression. The old things, which once had meant so very much to her, now held only half their meaning. The other half, she realized with heart-stopping regret, lay with Max.

It was, perhaps, a blessing when the matter of her troublesome telephoner took a turn for the worse. No longer would she be able to ignore an open-ended threat. For, now, she had a date, a point in time toward which her life, according to this as yet unknown menace, approached some equally as unknown climax.

The new development occurred during that first week in May, when everyone else had begun to walk a bit lighter, to smile a bit more gaily, to relax a bit more openly under the increasingly indulgent sun. She had returned home from work, only to have her phone ring within minutes of having dropped her briefcase, with a tired sigh, onto the kitchen table.

"Hello?"

"See, I know just when you get home, lady," the voice began, its satisfaction evident. As always, Laura fought the impulse to hang up on him. But the arguments of the police on the matter were correct; the longer she could keep the mystery man on the phone, the greater was the chance of tracing the call.

"Who is this?" Her voice was tired, indifferent.

"You should only know," the other went on, a sneering quality now in it which she'd never heard but alerted her slightly. "That would spoil the fun. No, lady, you'll be sweating it out by the time I'm done with you." He paused before delivering the punch line. "But, don't worry, there's not much longer to go, May the fifteenth. Don't forget. May the fifteenth."

That was all. He'd hung up. *May 15.* Why did that sound familiar to her, she asked herself, thinking of her own calendar for any coincidental dates or appointments that could have sparked the instant recognition. Automatically, she dialed Frank's number, then Sandy's, when no one answered the first. Under strict orders to report immediately any change in the status quo, she had not the courage to disobey, diligently repeating to the trooper, word for word, as close as she recalled it, the harrowing message she'd just received.

Yes, benumbed as she'd been during the past weeks, this most recent happening had succeeded in pricking her sensibilities. Whether it was that she'd been given a specific date, or it was the date itself that haunted her with its familiarity, Laura wasn't sure. But she had suddenly become uneasy.

Intent on reassurance, both the D.A. and the police stressed the advantage that each small bit of information—in this case, the date—gave them in their efforts. Yet as each day passed and each old file was searched and discarded, leads were as scarce as smiles on Laura's pale face.

The phone calls, coming now again nearly every night, were more varied. At times there was only the vague threat. At times there was mention of something Laura had done that day that the caller had observed. He might tell her what she'd been wearing, or where she'd eaten lunch, before reminding her of the fast approaching fifteenth of May.

The police detail around her was stepped up, patrol cars now passing at close intervals outside her house, often stopping across the street in silent vigil. Sandy had taken to picking her up in the morning and dropping her home at night, a habit which, despite her outward protest, gave her comfort. She found herself constantly looking about her, off to the side, back over her shoulder—hoping to see and recognize some misplaced face from the past come back to haunt her.

Through it all, she found great support, though no solace, in her friends. There was only one person who could have given her solace, and he was now gone from her life.

As her nerves began to fray, so seemingly did those of her nameless tormenter, as the middle of the month approached and the phone calls became even more frequent. The obsession with which this man had planned and was carrying out his cruel scheme had convinced Laura that his was a perverted mind, and one that held great potential for violence. The calls grew more angry, often obscene, and were dominated by a seething vengeance that thoroughly frightened her.

It occurred to her to pack up and leave until the ominous date had passed; Frank had even suggested as much, when the twelfth of May rolled around with no sign of a break in the case.

"Why don't you visit with Howard for a while. You could use the rest, and he'd love to have you in Chicago!" he had urged.

"No, Frank. I don't want to go to Chicago." She had dismissed the suggestion with undue petulance. The only place she could imagine herself escaping to was Rockport, and that thought irritated her all the more. She would never go to Rockport again . . . never! "And besides," she argued amid her annoyance, "I can't really run away from this man. He'd only follow me. He's gone to such efforts to do it all the time now," she added bitterly and with subtle accusation, "and your guys can't even find him!" Her eyes clouded over as she pondered the date once again. "May fifteenth—it rings a bell every time, but I just can't pinpoint it for the life of me . . ."

Frank echoed her frustration. "The fellows have been through the files of every case you've prosecuted since you've been in the office, and there is no significance that we can find to the date." His cheeks were at their ruddiest, his eyes emitting currents of worry through his glasses. "I think you should have a policewoman with you around the clock for the next few days."

"No! That's unnecessary." She argued vehemently. "He's building everything up to the fifteenth. He won't do anything before that." Deep inside she knew that only in her quiet, private times at home could she release the grief that periodically overtook her. To have someone, a stranger, with her every minute, would be stifling. Her pain of missing Max was a very deep and intimate one; it was enough of an effort to hide it when she was at work. To have to do so at home was tantamount to cruel and undue punishment.

"I hope not, Laura." Frank reluctantly acceded to her wish. "But, just remember, young lady, that I have the final say, and come the fifteenth you will go nowhere alone."

Laura could barely think that far—a mere three days—in advance; one day was about her limit. If she could get through a full day of work, a lonely evening, broken only by the horror of the telephone, and into bed, without a major spell of either bitterness, anger, or self-pity, she felt she'd done quite well.

On the night of the fourteenth, the phone call was at its most fevered and most revealing. "Time's almost up, lady. I'll show you, just like I showed those others. No woman is gonna make a fool of me!" He seethed in near-demented fashion. "You'll be sorry for what you did, lady. You can bet your boots on that. I'm gonna do to you just what I did to them." As always, he'd hung up in time to prevent tracing the call.

Just like the others, he had said. As the night passed, Laura racked her brain for some clue. *May the fifteenth. Just like the others.* It had to be a giveaway, yet she couldn't solve the mystery. She barely slept that night, though her door was bolted, as ordered, and a police car spent the night parked by her sidewalk. Although she'd been expecting it, she jumped when the doorbell rang the next morning, composing herself enough to greet the woman who would be accompanying her everywhere on this D-Day of sorts.

If she was a bundle of raw nerves when she left her apartment, quietly shadowed by her bodyguard, it was nothing compared to the terror she felt when, just before noon, she received the phone call at work. Never had he called her there before. But his own warped excitement had gotten out of hand.

"It's me, Miss Prosecutor," he enunciated mockingly. "We got a date later? You're gonna be pleased to see who I am finally. And believe me, you won't be disappointed." His voice held a stomach-wrenching blend of anger, violence, and sexuality. "Even nine years in that stinkin' hell hole of a prison didn't hurt my virility none." He laughed a sharp, ugly laugh. "Oh, yah, you'll get yours later."

Trembling when she hung up the phone, Laura sank into her chair and let the policewoman call her superiors to report this latest incident. *Nine years in prison. May the fifteenth. Just like the others.* One more piece to the puzzle, and it gave them nothing! They had known all along that it had had to be a work-related miscreant; Laura had never had enemies to speak of, certainly none capable of this kind of evil. Yet even knowing that the man had been in prison for nine years gave them no leads. After all, nine years ago, when this man had first been sent to jail, Laura had been a mere undergraduate.

It was a combustible combination of confusion, anger, and fear that exploded within Laura when Frank appeared in her office brief moments later insisting that they put a look-alike decoy in her place for the rest of the day. "No! Absolutely not! I've come this far, Frank, and I'm going to finally see who that maniac is! I'll have Shirley here with me all day; she can protect me when he finally makes his move!" Her blue eyes were wide and determined, her voice tremulous.

"I'm sorry, Laura. I don't want to take that chance. I told you once: *I* have the final say. You're getting out of here. I've already sent for your stand-in. She looks like you. When you've switched clothes, this monster will be easily duped."

"And if he doesn't?" she challenged brashly. "Then do I wait for him to start all over again?" A quick glance told her that the proposed decoy had, in fact, arrived, along with several other nonuniformed policemen. Laura knew her argument would have to be strong enough to conquer this army that had invaded her small office. "Frank"—she lowered her voice and spoke shakily to her boss—"I have to get this over, once and for all. I'm so well watched that I won't be hurt, believe me, but if he catches any hint of a switch, he's apt to cancel the whole thing." The azure of her eyes brightened in frantic pleading. "I can't go through this again. We need to get him out in the open—finally!"

For an instant Laura felt as though she were the demented one, standing in the center of a circle of silently sad and sympathetic caretakers. It seemed that everything she had so steadily built up in her life was about to crumble. Then out of the soundless maelstrom, a deep voice broke through, strongly velvet-rich and familiar.

"You're absolutely right, Laura, we do need to get him out into the open. But that is the business of these people." Dark brown eyes intently scanned the ring of faces before returning to rest determinedly on the one that had whirled to face him. "You're coming with me."

Her breath caught in her throat as her gaze locked with that of the man to whom she'd confessed her love, in a heartbreaking moment of torment and humiliation over a month ago. She'd not seen him since, and had no desire to see him now. For with his dark handsomeness and inherently compelling personage came a renewal of that same shame and degradation she'd suffered at his hands on that last day.

Helpless to understand what he was doing here now, casually dressed as he was in an open-necked cotton shirt, cuffs rolled to the elbows, and jeans, her horror-stricken gaze flew to the D.A.'s face, itself tense and rigid. "Frank?" she whispered hoarsely, a gut feeling of betrayal engulfing her. "What's *he* doing here?" In a moment of dismay she feared that she'd poured her heart out to Frank only to have it turned and used against her.

The politician pushed his glasses farther up on his nose, then smoothed down the thin gray hairs on the top of his head. "He's been kept informed of the developments, Laura. You knew that. But I had no idea he'd show up." He kept his voice low, given the more personal undercurrents of the subject matter. Now he moved his gaze above and behind Laura to where Max stood, implicitly questioning on his own.

Laura felt a steel grip seize her arm. "Let's go, Laura. You have to change first, I stopped by your apartment to pick up some clothes for several days' vacation, so it will be no problem for you to give your things to this kind woman." His head tilted in the direction of the newly arrived policewoman.

Totally disbelieving of this latest turn of events, Laura allowed herself to be guided out of the office, away from the politely curious looks of both the plain-clothesmen and the policewoman. Once in the hall, however, she rebelled, in a spurt of awareness, catching Max off guard and pulling away from him with a jerk.

"I'm not going anywhere with you." Every muscle in her body trembled, yet her fists were clenched and a grimness overwhelmed her features.

To her dismay, Max was as tense and grim. "You're coming with me *now*. I've threatened before, and I'll do it—I'll carry you out of here bodily, if need be." Laura knew only too well, from other, infinitely more tender moments, of his ability to bodily move her. He was thoroughly intimidating, towering above her. Reflexively, she moved back against the wall.

Her voice was low and came through gritted teeth as the memory of her past humiliation stirred a seething anger within her. "I won't go with you, Max. I'll leave but not with you."

Before she'd taken another breath, Max stepped forward to put both hands on the wall on either side of her, his solid form a hair's breadth from her stiffened one, his breath fanning her hair in painful reminder of past intimacies. His tone was quiet yet unyielding. Here was the embodiment of a stubbornness she'd once only imagined.

"Don't make me hurt you any more that I already have, Laura. It's about time we both acted our age. But that we'll get to later. The immediate problem is getting you away from this mess. Now"—he stood back a bit—"I'm going to call that decoy out here, and you and she can go into the ladies' room and change clothes. I've got your bag right here." He pointed to the small overnight bag, which she instantly recognized as the one that had been stored in the spare room when she'd left the apartment that morning.

"What business did you have going to my

209

home? You've got no right, Max—" The ongoing drama had driven her to near hysterics.

"I've got every right in the world! Now do you go willingly, or do I have to use force?"

Laura let her chin drop onto her chest as she took several deep breaths. *This whole thing is ludicrous,* she told herself over and over, trying to grasp what was happening but falling short of any understanding.

"I'll change and leave here, but I'm not going with you," she repeated in a final bid for dignity. She hadn't lifted her head, but heard Max's half-whispered oath. Roughly, he took hold of her arm and held it as he moved back to the door of her office to interrupt the intensely serious huddle.

Laura wasn't sure how she found herself, ten minutes later, sitting in the front seat of the shiny brown Mercedes. She'd had every intention of escaping Max's presence as soon as she'd changed into the blouse, jeans, and sandals she'd found, among other things, in her bag, yet he'd been waiting right outside the ladies' room and had taken her nearly bruised arm once more, overriding her objections that he had no right, that he was hurting her, that he was nothing but a selfish, sadistic bastard.

"She looked pretty good in your clothes, that decoy did," he commented easily as the car headed out of Northampton. "And very much like you." As though to further remove them from the fast-receding scene, he deftly reached over, and before she realized what he had in mind, had removed the two strategic pins that had held the coil of her hair neatly in place. The damage was done, even as she batted his hand away, combing her hair out over her shoulders with her slender fingers. Glaring as she was at the passing scenery, she missed the self-satisfied grin on Max's face.

Laura was in no mood for conversation. Inwardly, she agreed with Max that the resemblance was remarkable between her and the decoy Frank and Sandy had dug up. They must have been planning this for quite some time! Sandy . . . where had *he* been during that mortifying few moments in her office?

"Did you and Sandy dream up this little getaway together?" she burst out, now suspicious, then shocked at the possibility of treason from that source.

Max never took his eyes from the road, his expression half-hidden from her own suspicious gaze. "Let's get one thing straight. I didn't plan anything with anyone. No one knew I'd be driving in this morning . . . least of all myself," he added in a much softer, more self-directed tone. "But, to answer your suspicions, I *have* been in touch with Chatfield. He's not a bad sort, once he gets over that innate distrust of his. Boy," he reminisced, "did he let me have it, at one point there." A smile played at the corner of his strong lips, but Laura was in no playful mood.

"Served you right," she snapped, then stiffened as her eyes returned to the road. "Where are you taking me?" The car had taken a wide turn onto the ramp leading to the Mass Pike.

"Boston."

"Why Boston?" Her distraught mind flew back to the last time she'd been in Boston, and a shudder coursed through her.

"We're going to my town house."

"I'm not—"

"You have no choice!" he thundered. "Now if we can't talk civilly, I don't care to talk at all. Just keep still until we get there."

That was exactly what she did, keeping her face averted for most of the trip, struggling with the warring emotions within her. From that real and violent threat of danger this morning to this real but very different threat this afternoon . . . where would it end? She still loved Max, as she'd known she always would. But that fact had been made even more clear to her when he'd so unexpectedly appeared earlier in her office. Strangely, as much as she had fought his presence, she did feel more at east regarding the danger posed by her faceless stalker. In fact, she mused amid the dilemma of Maxwell Kraig, this was the first thought she'd given to that other menace since Max had arrived. But where was she going in life? Where would this trip lead? What further humiliation did Max have in store for her?

Closing her eyes against the quagmire, she drifted into a doze of sheer exhaustion, only to come to life with a start when the car slowed at the turnpike exit and delved onto the more crowded streets of Boston. Her embarrassed glance at Max was met by a surprisingly grim glare. "You look exhausted! It's no wonder you fell asleep. What have you done to yourself in the past month? You're pale, thin, overtired—that's what I'd call a keen instinct for survival," he barked sarcastically.

Wary of only angering him more—and fearful of that, since she was literally at his mercy—Laura rested her elbow against the door and jammed a clenched fist against her mouth. "Well?" he prodded. "Have you been running around with every man in sight?" With remarkably little concentration, he turned onto Charles Street and headed toward Beacon Hill.

"You're disgusting," she seethed, turning her blue gaze on the enigmatic man beside her, no longer able to curb her own explosive anger. "I haven't been anywhere for the last month. If I'm pale, it's because I work during all of the daylight hours. If I'm thin, it's because I don't care to eat. And if I'm tired, it's because I can't sleep at night. But you . . . you're the one who's probably been sowing enough wild oats for the two of us! *You're the only sexually dangerous person I know—*" In the back of her mind a bell rang. The dawn broke. She gasped at what she'd just said, as the pieces to the puzzle finally fell into place. So immersed was she in the unfolding discovery that she totally missed the broad grin, for the first time more relaxed, that spread across his face. "My God," she whispered breathlessly, "that's it. Sexually dangerous . . . I stood in on that hearing . . ."

The smile vanished from his manly features as Max turned into the driveway abutting his town house and drove through to the central courtyard. "Laura, what are you saying?"

She closed her eyes and put several shaky fingers to her forehead in a desperate attempt at recalling the details. "I can't remember his name . . . it was right after I started working in the D.A.'s office . . . you know, those periodic hearings to determine whether an inmate is still to be considered sexually dangerous . . ." She paused, remembering more clearly the facts of the case now. A large, very gentle hand settled on her shoulder.

"Go on," he urged softly. She cringed at her own words as she did so.

"He had raped and brutally beaten three women. Always on May fifteenth. Only the last one was ever prosecuted, and he was convicted. He came up each year for hearings, since his release from prison was contingent on his being found no longer sexually dangerous. He'd served already five, no, six years in prison, I think, and could have been let out at any time. I happened to have subbed for someone else that day, a lawyer who left soon afterward." She took a gulping breath as the words flowed. "When the judge sent him back to prison that day, he burst out into a raging tantrum. His behavior only reinforced the psychiatrists' reports and our own recommendations. I guess he resented me more for being a woman than for sending him back to that hell hole, as he called it on the phone this morning." She looked helplessly at Max. "You know how cruelly the prison population treats sex offenders." She shuddered again, oblivious of the comforting caress the strong hand had begun on her shoulders. "I was only filling in on the case, so it wouldn't have even been on the list of cases the state police searched." She shook her head in dismay. "I should have seen it sooner. Damn it, I should have seen it! The clues were all there!" She fell silent, stunned by the implication of what this ex-convict had had in mind for her.

"Come on, baby, I've got to call your boss. They still have that pretty decoy to protect."

Spent of all resistance, she followed him quietly into the house, huddling into a corner of a plush sofa as he called Northampton and passed on her

214

discovery. Only when he came to sit in the deep armchair opposite her did she recall her present, more soulful dilemma.

Ten

"Are you all right?" The concern in his voice was mirrored in his dark brown eyes. He made no move to close the distance between them, merely studied her intently. She avoided his gaze, letting her blue eyes drift randomly about this room which, in its understated elegance, bore the undeniably familiar stamp of the owner.

She began in a tremulous voice, her senses confused, her composure negligible. "I feel . . . overwhelmed. These past few months have thrown me . . ." Some tiny thread of reason reminded her that by all rights she should be angry at this man, not only for what he'd done to her in the past, but for having dragged her away from the center of action this very morning. But all resentment, all bitterness had vanished. He had a knack of doing that to her, each and every time. Yet in so many ways he would have been very good for her, knowing just how to comfort her, to humor her, to exert pressure when pressure was called for. If only . . .

"I love you, Laura." So sure was she that the words had been in her own mind, Laura bowed her head lower, drawing further into herself as the agony of loving flared again. When the words came a second time, they were nearer—soft, intimate, and heartfelt. "I love you."

Unable to believe what she'd heard, she raised her head to find Max squatting before her, his eyes level with hers, his hands resting on the cushions on either side of her. "Please hear me, Laura," he begged in a near whisper. "I love you."

Words eluded her. It was another trick, she rued frantically, incredulously, her eyes widening, her gaze searching the ceiling for some shred of reality to which she could cling. It was impossible that he should love her, after all he'd done!

Sensing her thoughts, Max straightened and walked to the window. "You were right about so very many things. I have been a bastard, and you have every right to despise me. But I'd like a chance to explain before you pass final judgment." His hands were thrust into his pants pockets as he kept his back to her. Laura was unable to move, her sight dominated by the broad expanse of blue-clothed back that faced her.

"I had no intention of falling in love," he began slowly, but with the conviction of having rehearsed the speech repeatedly in his mind. "I had my career, my social life, my celebrity status. I don't know exactly when it happened, but by the end of that weekend in Rockport, it was a fait accompli. I knew, then, that I loved you. But I had no idea how to handle it. We had the Stallway case coming up, which meant so much to you. I couldn't bear the thought of your not prosecuting it. I tried to avoid seeing you, but that backfired. Then, when you showed up here . . ." He paused as they both recalled the time she'd driven to this town house.

"Those things I said, Laura, they weren't true.

I *never* thought of you only in the physical sense. You have to believe that." He turned and came to stand before her, the inherent soul-touch of his chocolate gaze reinforcing his words. Then, as though he felt awkward towering above and talking down, he lowered his long frame to the sofa, careful to leave space between them. There was only earnestness in the eyes that pleaded so uncharacteristically. Laura's own face had frozen into a mask of pain, wanting to believe him . . . yet afraid.

"It was your spirit that first attracted me, your wit, your intelligence. You were so many different women—the ultimate professional, the sophisticate, the do-gooder, the free spirit. You were the most enchanting woman I'd ever met. And you were beautiful. I knew that you excited me physically, but that was not the major thing. Until . . ." He hesitated, unsure as to how far he could push her composure. ". . . until you let me make love to you."

Burned by the memory of the passion that had raged between them, she averted her eyes from his. But strong fingers gently guided her jaw back. "No, Laura, don't look away from me. I want you to see what I'm saying." His eyes captured hers in such a mesmerizing intensity that she was unable to look elsewhere. There was a heart-rending tenderness there that held her prisoner. His voice bore an underlying huskiness as he continued.

"When I made love to you, when you made love to me, it was an experience so far above the purely physical! I guess that's when I knew that I loved you. I've been no celibate, Laura, for the past twenty years. I've had my share of women;

I'm sure you knew that. But never did I feel anything akin to what we shared. Ours was a physical joining made spiritual."

He sighed, combing his fingers roughly through his thick mane of brown hair. "And if you accuse me again of sounding like I'm before a jury, I'll strangle you." She blushed then, recalling the hurt that had prompted that vicious accusation. "That's better," he crooned, suddenly more relaxed. "I've been waiting for that blush. You look better with a little color in your cheeks." He raised a finger in a light caress of the spot in mention.

Laura had neither moved nor spoken. Yet she was aware that the horror of these past weeks had begun to recede. For the first time in days she felt a lessening of the pain that had so seized her mind and body.

But Max had not finished. "I was so proud of you during the trial. You were professional, dignified, quick—all the things I've always respected in a fellow lawyer." His face held that respect, and the pain within Laura eased even more. "Then, after the trial, I simply lost control. I was so pleased that it was over, that we could finally be together again. But when I found that you hated me for everything I'd done, I couldn't begin to cope."

In a moment of self-disgust, he grimaced, then bolted up and stormed back to the window. "I nearly raped you, Laura." Every bit of pain that she'd harbored over the weeks had settled in Max's voice. "I nearly raped you!" He put his hands on his hips and looked skyward in a gesture of despair. "I don't think I'll ever forgive myself for that!"

To glory in the pain of another was contrary to Laura's nature, yet it was Max's very pain that convinced her, once and for all, of the truth of his words and his feelings. Hope met joy in a blessed awakening within her. Slowly and silently, she rose from the sofa and crossed the room to lightly slip her arms through his and lock her slender fingers together, pulling herself gently against him, resting her joy-flushed cheek on the muscled strength of his back. She could hear the loud drumming of his heart, a life-infusing pulse to her, as she unconsciously tightened her grip. There was one last question she wanted to ask, needing only that last bit of reassurance. Her voice was not much more than a whisper.

"Why did you come out to get me today, Max?"

His body had begun to relax as she'd embraced him. Now she felt his fingers tentatively cover hers as he took a deep, shuddering breath. "I couldn't leave you out there, Laura, with that maniac on the loose. I knew that today was to be the day, I just couldn't let you stay. Frank hinted that he'd planned to get you out, but knowing your streak of hardheadedness, I figured he might have trouble." Her obvious smile against his back urged him on. "You may have been furious, Laura, but I had no intention of letting the woman I love remain in that kind of danger."

Never had Laura heard such beautiful words. Max had to pry her fingers apart in order to turn and face her. There was an infinite silence as they looked at each other, and when he finally spoke, his plea was from the heart, brimming with hope.

"Once you said you loved me, Laura. Is there

enough forgiveness in you to begin to love again?" Her now luminous eyes didn't flinch under his directness.

"I never stopped loving you, Max," she declared softly, as she raised a faintly trembling hand to trace his cheekbone and the line of his jaw, now eased.

His firm lips kissed the tips of her fingers as they passed by on their wonder-filled journey. "I've missed you so much, baby. You'll never know!" he murmured with feeling.

There was a sly twinkle in her own eye when Laura nodded vigorously. "Oh, I know. Why do you think I've worked myself ragged, eaten practically nothing, and gotten little sleep?"

His grin was the one she'd always melted beneath. "I was hoping, in my own perverse way, that that was the reason. But I intend to remedy those problems from here on in."

"Oh?"

"Yes!" he growled playfully, tightening the arms which now encircled her waist. "For starters, you're spending the rest of the week here. I picked up those things at your apartment, and anything else you need we can shop for together."

Sudden suspicion stirred her. "How did you manage to get into my apartment? Either you picked the lock or you beguiled Mrs. Daniels."

A quiver of excitement passed through her limbs at the beaming smile sent her way. How good it was to see him happy, she mused, knowing that to be the only sunshine she truly needed. Devilment was written over his dark features. "I'm afraid I must plead guilty to the latter. Actually, Mrs. Daniels was a pushover. It only took one good smile."

"Hmmm, that's all it ever takes," she reflected aloud, blatantly referring to her own susceptibility.

As though in retaliation of her quip, he did it again. This time her insides quaked with the stirrings of more heady beguilement. Her fingers snaked around the column of his neck to wind into the thickness of his hair, subtly pressing his head forward.

"Kiss me, Max," she urged in a bold whisper. "I've waited so long." He needed no further urging, lowering his head until his lips, firm and cool, met hers, soft and warm, in a soul-reaching caress filled with gentleness and love. As his hands molded her pliant body ever closer, she shuddered with desire, a current that flowed from her body to his and back in wordless communion. Max's eyes were filled with the same smoldering ember as hers, when their lips finally fell apart.

"I love you," he rasped against her forehead, crushing her against his body moments before he lifted her off her feet and into his arms.

"Where are you taking me?" she shrieked in mock rebellion, clinging to his neck with suddenly reborn strength.

He'd left the living room and had begun to climb the flight of stairs two at a time, her weight but a token in his arms, before he answered. "We're going to bed. *My* bed. I've dreamed of making fast and furious love to you there for the past three months, and I'm not waiting a minute longer."

"Aren't you going to show me around your home first?" she protested coyly.

"Later!" He continued climbing.

"Aren't you going to feed this poor undernourished woman?" she teased.

"Later!"

"Aren't you even going to see that I make up for all the sleep I've lost over you?"

"Later!"

Laura's features were illuminated by the soft light of love. "Thank God!" She exhaled an exaggerated sigh of relief just before she was dropped atop the velours blanket that covered the bed in which she had imagined herself lying beside the man who now joined her in an age-old ritual of passionate delight.

Among the many realities that ceased to exist during this precious time of rediscovery was the drama that had played itself out in Northampton late that afternoon. It wasn't until long after dark, when Max finally chose to answer his telephone, that they learned that the man who had unsuccessfully attempted to attack Laura's judo-trained look-alike was, indeed, the man who had once been declared sexually dangerous by a young, attractive, and very perceptive female prosecutor. Safely and permanently behind bars, this man had no further place in Laura's thoughts, her every energy devoted to the one who had captured her heart.

The sun had cascaded in red-orange trickles across the Charles when, much later Max called Laura back to him from her perch. As she returned to the bed, his eyes surveyed the wonder of her femininity, fulfilled at last.

"So warm and fresh," he murmured huskily, reaching out to touch the ivory smoothness of a shapely hip as she slid onto the crisp sheets and nestled against his hairy manliness.

"Spring is finally here," she mused dreamily. "It's been a long time coming." The deeper meaning of her words was clear, Max having shared the rebirth of their oneness. Now as his eyes roamed the gentle curves of her body, she knew of delicate green buds blooming into sun-graced maturity. Ripples of ecstasy surged as his hand paved a gentle trail from shoulder to breast to rib cage, coming to rest in splayed possession of her flat belly.

"You know," he began in a worshipful croon, his eyes filled with future imaginings as his words traced the past, "I'd half hoped you *were* pregnant. The thought of your carrying our child pleases me."

Long-suppressed guilt quickly surfaced. "Max, you have to know that I didn't mean what I said that day on the phone," she burst out in urgent confession. "I could never have harmed our child. Never!" She drew back and turned her face toward his as she spoke, her rounded eyes proclaiming her honesty. "It would be a very precious experience, to bear your child."

He smiled mischievously. "My children."

"Your children!"

With passion-inspired gruffness, he pulled her head back against his shoulder. "I think we're getting ahead of ourselves. Will you mind terribly being married to a lawyer? I won't!"

"But if I'm going to raise all these children, there will hardly be time for law—"

"Whoa! You're jumping the gun again. In the first place, I think we can wait a bit for the little ones. There's too much I want to do with you alone. Secondly, I will not let you give up your career!" The vehemence in his voice precluded any argument, though he underscored his determination more gently. "You're too good a lawyer for that, Laura. And looking at the skillful way you do just about everything else, I've no doubt that you could very comfortably combine motherhood and a career. After all, what better way to have a totally flexible schedule than to be in partnership with your husband?"

Admiration intermixed with adoration as she gazed up at his brown-eyed brilliance. "You've got it all planned, haven't you?"

He grinned. "Not all. I haven't figured out how I'm going to tell Frank that his best lawyer will be leaving him. I haven't figured out how we're going to break the news to those sassy kids of yours. And I haven't figured out how I'm going to concede to Chatfield that he was right, that I was a fool to risk losing you."

"Did Sandy really say that?"

"Ummm . . . that and more, and in much more picturesque language, I might add."

A triumphant giggle erupted through love-rouged lips. "Good boy, Sandy!"

Max delivered a playful pat to Laura's bare bottom before melting into tenderness. Firm lips brushed her forehead, long fingers followed to gently smooth a loose strand of black hair away from her face, then trailed down her cheek to her throat, where lay the small gold heart and its throbbing ruby.

"How fitting that this should be the only thing you're wearing. I didn't think you would have had it on, after all that happened . . ."

A mere whisper answered him. "It was all I had of you. Even when I thought I never wanted to see you again, I couldn't take it off. You were everything I'd always wanted, Max. I knew that you'd always have my love, but I feared this was all I'd ever have of you." Her fingers met his at the heart they shared.

Any reminiscent pain was blotted out beneath a soul-reaching kiss, as Max forever stilled those old fears. When he reluctantly released her lips, it was to speak warmly against her forehead. "You were right, you know, when you accused me of being afraid. I'd never been able to see it before. I was afraid of making the ultimate commitment."

His moment of self-reproach was broken by Laura's loving quest. "And now? Are you still afraid?"

The fierceness of his response thrilled her. "Yes! I'm terrified of facing a life of emptiness such as I had a taste of this past month. Yes." He gave a nodding confirmation in answer to her stare of wonderment. "I felt the same pain you did."

This time it was Laura who stilled his voice with her kiss, sweet and compassionate. "I love you," she murmured against his lips, moments before he rolled over with a growl to playfully pin her to the bed. His voice was husky with arousal. "You know, Madame Prosecutor, my client got off lightly. I've drawn a life sentence."

"Some prison you've got here," she drawled, impishly running the sole of her foot the length of a delightfully rough-textured shin.

Her mischief was contagious, bringing a naughty gleam to his eye. "Hmmm . . . the nicest thing about it is that conjugal visits are required."

Her voice lowered seductively. "Must I be a wife to qualify?"

" 'Fraid so."

"Then you'll just have to marry me, because I'm not leaving!" It was a joyous declaration, a vow before the others.

"Enchanting tigress, I wouldn't dream of letting you go," he murmured against the bright sheen of her hair, as his arms imprisoned her in love-bound shackles, from which she prayed never, never to be freed.

IF YOU HAVE ENJOYED READING
THIS LARGE PRINT BOOK AND
YOU WOULD LIKE MORE
INFORMATION ON HOW TO
ORDER A WHEELER LARGE PRINT
BOOK, PLEASE WRITE TO:

WHEELER PUBLISHING, INC.
P.O. BOX 531
ACCORD, MA 02018-0531